TALES OF A BLACK THERAPIST

TALES
OF A
BLACK
THERAPIST

CHRIS GAMBLE

To my parents, Bob and Donna, for their support and encouraging my love of reading since childhood. To my brother, Jeff, for always having my back.

"He began to have a dim feeling that, to attain his place in the world, he must be himself, and not another."

—W.E.B. Du Bois, The Souls of Black Folk

CHAPTER
ONE

Once again, he'd have to find another way in.

He clutched the knob with his left hand while gripping the key with the other, turning until it felt like the key would snap, leaving the door locked forever. The weekly afternoons Drew spent at the Rosedale Community Center were some of his favorites, but the much-in-need-of-renovation building too often turned up inconveniences like this. He was already running behind, leaving himself little time to prepare for his first session. Breaking the frosted glass window to his office door had crossed his mind before, if only he weren't so sure the glass wouldn't get repaired either.

So instead, he moved the gray messenger bag slung over his shoulder and reached into his side pocket for his wallet. He took his credit card out and angled it between the door and frame, right above the lock mechanism. Slowly shimmying and sliding the card down, he found just enough space to wedge it beside the latch bolt and pop the door open. He raised his fist in exaggerated excitement when a voice from behind startled him.

"Now don't you let any of the kids see that little trick of yours, Mr. Gaines. You of all people know how impressionable they can be."

He turned back to see Tina Ramos, the RCC Youth Program Director, smirking at him with a hand on her hip, dark curls bouncing as she tilted her head to the side. Always a hands-on leader ready to engage with the kids, her crispy white sneakers had kept her undetectable during Drew's low-level offense. Her footwear reminded him of when they first met. She had been on the RCC basketball court, taking on a trio of young, overly confident boys on her own. Weaving between them with swift between-the-leg dribbles, fluidly transitioning into a smooth backspin and layup, Tina's days as an athlete hadn't seemed too far behind her. Since then, he'd turned down all of her challenges, comfortable to keep their friendship off the hardwood.

"Don't worry, I think you're the only one who saw." He smiled with a slight shrug. "Besides, what am I supposed to do while waiting for someone to fix this thing? I'm a busy man." He tugged at the lapels of his navy-blue cardigan, trying to look the part of a seasoned professional.

"Yes, in high demand as always, Mr. Gaines," Tina replied, teasing him with a mock bow. "I'll leave you to it, then." She waved as she turned down the hallway toward her office. At her office door she pretended to fumble with the knob, using her fingernail to "pick" the lock. She smiled back at Drew before stepping out of view.

Drew entered his office, placing his bag on the floor and draping his cardigan on the back of his desk chair. Stress made him sweat, and he could feel his underarms starting to get hot beneath his t-shirt. The teens he worked with always teased him for wearing the cardigan anyway. They said it looked like some kind of therapist uniform. He'd remind them that he was indeed a real therapist, to no avail. He remembered how important style was at their age, so he kept a good sense of humor about it.

He took his laptop from his bag and opened it on the desk. While waiting for it to power up, he reached for his cell phone in the cardigan pocket hanging next to him. A text notification flashed on the screen. He must not have felt the vibration while fumbling with the door.

Tapping on the text, he read the message.

JD:

Sorry Mr. G. I gotta miss my session today. I got in trouble at school and sent home early so Mom won't let me leave the house.

Drew scrunched his eyes closed, pinching the top of his nose as he let out a sigh. Looks like he'd been in a rush for nothing. He stressed to all of his clients' parents not to cancel therapy sessions as punishment. School troubles were perfect material for a constructive session, but he was also well aware that Moms had the last say, so he simply texted back that they could catch up next week.

Just as Drew was about to login to his laptop, a knock sounded on the window of his open door. Looking up, he spotted another one of his clients, Lawrence, poking his head into the office. "You free Mr. G?"

Since he was only at the community center once a week, Drew let it be known to all his clients that they could drop by for quick check-ins whenever he was free. With his only scheduled session now canceled, time was in abundance.

"Sure, Lo, come on in." Early on, Lawrence told Drew to use his nickname. His friends gave it to him because it reflected his "lowkey" personality.

Lo closed the door behind him and put his backpack down before slumping into the dark green cushioned chair in the corner. "Bruh, Coach is tryna kick me off the team." His black hoodie stayed draped over his eyes as he rubbed his head back and forth with one hand, seemingly trying to caress the stress out of his brain.

"You told me you've been going to every practice. What's going on?" Drew asked. Football was one of the most important things in Lo's life. The consistency and predictability of the sport stood in contrast to so much of what he'd experienced in his turbulent sixteen years.

"I do go to practice now. I just don't always be on time." A smirk twitched across his face before fading into the shadow of his hood. One thing Drew had learned about Lo was that under his chill demeanor hid a sense of humor that could bite as much as it could warm those around him.

"Mmhmm. It seems like there's a reason why. Care to share?" Drew prodded.

"Coach keeps saying some corny stuff like, 'You're too busy trying to be a player instead of learning the playbook.' I don't know what he's talking about, man." Lo snorted out a stifled laugh. "I only have one girl so that's not really being much of a player."

Drew pulled his lips in and bit down to stop his own laughter. "So, this one girl is taking up all of your time?"

Lo opened his eyes, cutting them right at Drew. The hard glare disappeared as his gaze drifted down. His eyes seemed ready to pop as he jerked up and forward to the edge of the chair. "Wait, Mr. G are those church shoes on your feet?" He rolled back, cackling hysterically. "Just get one of those old wireless earpieces and you'll look like one of my uncles."

No matter how hard he tried, Drew's wardrobe couldn't escape the roast radar of his young clients. They were good. "Okay, okay, I'll give you that one," he said, shaking his head and holding his hands up in surrender. "Now, what would you like to do about this football problem?"

Lo shrugged, settling back into his previously shrouded presentation.

"Clearly, you're not giving up on it since you keep going to practice," Drew reflected. "And you also seem to be enjoying this new person in your life. We talk a lot about the future in here. What it means for you to develop into an adult and take on those responsibilities. How do you think this fits in?" Drew was well aware of Lo's motivation to prove his doubters wrong. To show he could succeed in ways no one expected of him.

"I guess this is one of those situations where I have to find a balance," Lo said. "Adults have to figure out how to focus on their jobs and families all the time. This is just my version of it."

Drew nodded in agreement.

"Alright, well I better get home before my Granny gets on me." Lo picked up his backpack and dapped up Drew before turning to leave. "I'll catch you later, Mr. G."

"See you next week. Keep me updated on how football goes." Drew stood and closed the door behind Lawrence, pleased with how the check-in had gone.

Before any others could drop in, he decided to catch up on some administrative work. Outside of the weekly visits to the RCC, he had a growing private practice that kept him busy. Writing progress notes for his sessions was a time-consuming task, but the stream of emails he received seemed infinite, so he checked those first. Going through his unread messages, Drew spotted one from earlier in the afternoon with a university email address that caught his eye. It'd been a while since he'd heard from any schools, so he hoped for good news, holding in a breath as he read.

Mr. Gaines,

Hi, I'm a student at Greenview State and I saw a flyer yesterday for your group during my professor's office hours. I'm not sure if I was supposed to see it, but I'm really interested. I hope you don't mind me reaching out like this. The flyer said you're at the community center on Wednesdays. I work around the corner from there so I can stop by right after my shift is done. Maybe 5:30?

Best,
Amir

Drew exhaled, scratching his head at the message. At the beginning of the fall semester, he'd gotten in contact with a few nearby universities' undergrad Psychology programs to let them know he was starting a mentoring group. The group was intended for Black male upperclassmen who either expressed interest in becoming therapists or showed promise for contributing something unique to the field. He'd asked program faculty to select the students based on their own observations and connect them to him so he could figure out if they were a good fit for the structure he had in mind. It was close to midterm time and he'd only received two referrals so far. He wasn't sold on either of them. He needed at least ten members by the end of the semester to start the group in the spring, so he didn't have the luxury to stall. The fact that this student was reaching out directly was intriguing.

With the deadline drawing nearer, Drew decided to reply.

Hey Amir,

I'll be at the RCC for another few hours so feel free to stop by. I look forward to chatting.

Kindly,
Drew Gaines, LPC

Feeling embarrassingly desperate, he hit send. He'd wanted professors to select the students themselves in order to act as a kind of filter in his vetting process, but with the pace and quality of referrals so far, he felt it wouldn't hurt to give Amir a chance.

Every time Drew thought about starting the mentoring group, waves of nervous excitement hit him. At times he wondered if he was dreaming too big. Mentoring was nothing groundbreaking, yet he knew this was the path toward something truly impactful. He knew all too well what it felt like to walk down an unfamiliar road with no map, no sense of direction. He hoped to be a guide who could keep aspiring Black therapists on track.

As time passed, Drew worked through his unread emails, about half of his progress notes, and two cups of coffee. Suddenly, another knock rapped on his office door. "Come in," he said, recalling in the moment he was likely presenting a challenge rather than an invite. The slim shadow standing beyond the window wiggled the knob back and forth, not budging the door even slightly. "I got ya." Drew scooted back from his desk and came to the door, a quick pull removing the obstacle between him and the unknown figure.

"Pretty good security system you got there." The deep voice betrayed the boyish smile on the face standing at eye-level across from Drew. "You're Mr. Gaines, right? Someone at the front pointed me to your office."

"Yes, that's me," Drew answered. "And you must be Amir. Right on time," he said, looking at his watch. They shook hands as Drew motioned to the chair Lo was in earlier. Amir's black tracksuit had a single stripe going down the sides that nearly matched the cushioning. As he passed by, a pin on his backpack caught Drew's eye. Something about the symbol was familiar, but he couldn't quite place it.

"Yeah, I pass by the RCC on my way to the sneaker store where I work, so I knew it'd be easy to come through today," Amir said.

"I was surprised to see your email earlier, but my schedule cleared out unexpectedly so it was no problem squeezing you in," Drew explained.

"Sorry to just barge into your inbox like that," Amir said, nervously scratching the side of his head. "My dad always tells me to go for what I want, so I figured it was worth a try."

Drew closed his laptop and moved it aside so he could focus on his new guest. "Tell me how that happened. I've been following up with a few schools for recruits without much luck. Seems like you took matters into your own hands."

Amir sighed. "It's Ms. Perino, my Social Psych professor. I was in her office when I saw your flyer sticking out of a pile of papers. I'm not really sure how she feels about me, so instead of asking about it, I snuck a quick picture when our meeting was over, took some time to think about it, and then sent you the message."

"What makes you think this professor doesn't like you?" Drew asked.

"I don't know if it's that straightforward," Amir began. "I mean, she's cool and all, it's just the class itself. We're in there learning about how people make decisions and why people react to situations the way they do. But

I always feel like the examples are based on white people's lives. The guys who came up with all the theories are white. And Ms. Perino's white too, so I don't think she likes the way I challenge what she's teaching."

"Can you give me an example?" Drew asked.

Amir paused for a moment. "There was this time when she was teaching us about how when a crowd of people witness something bad, for instance, the responsibility to do something gets diffused among the crowd. Basically, the more people present, the less likely someone is to help or something like that. She said that's why certain communities have a 'no snitching' policy. Of course, I told her she was wrong and that her explanation ignored things like police violence and mass incarceration. She got mad at that."

Drew nodded. "Sounds like things could get a little tense between you two." He'd wanted the professors of the programs he was in contact with to be filters but had overlooked the potential for problematic gatekeeping. Maybe that explained why the first two referrals hadn't panned out so well.

Regardless of the class subject, or the grade level for that matter, Black students most times had to wish to have their worldviews reflected in their lessons. Before college, it was up to parents to convince school boards that Black perspectives are not special interests, but core parts of a comprehensive education for all students. Once guys like Amir made it to university campuses, the uphill battle continued to make their experiences heard and recognized as important and necessary. This is what Drew heard in Amir's dissatisfaction. He also understood the risk at hand when standing up for the truth. It sparked some of his own memories.

"You know, I'm reminded of my own experiences in grad school," Drew said. "I was set on getting my Master's in Counseling, excited to learn the skills to help people. The most important lessons I ended up learning weren't in the curriculum though. Do you mind if I share a couple stories with you?"

"Sure," Amir perked up. "I'm interested."

TALE #1: MISTAKEN IDENTITY

We spotted the only other Black student in the classroom. He looked at Cal and me through Malcolm X-style frames and gave a subtle downward nod, the kind designed for only us to see while it ducked under the radar in the sea of white. Couldn't let everyone know that we did in fact keep count of every Black person in the room when in predominantly white spaces.

It felt odd enough that Cal and I were walking in together. I gravitated to him so quickly at the new student orientation a couple weeks before, some students asked if we knew each other from undergrad. To be honest, it wasn't just that we were both Black that drew me to Cal. I was jealous of him in a way. Where I hesitated, he spoke with self-assurance. I was still seeking, while he knew who he was. It didn't take long for me to convince myself I could acquire his cool confidence by befriending him.

Cal and I scanned the classroom, noticing there were no seats near the other Black student, so we scooted down the far aisle of desks to a spot near the back corner. I imagined us drifting off into the white sea, wishing we had something to tether us to the one anchor of familiarity in the room. Perhaps this was for the best in order to avoid any assumptions about the three of us sitting together.

"Multicultural Counseling," the first course of the semester, seemed to be a popular one. Cal and I got the last open slots during registration.

"I mean, it's a required course, but the way it filled up so fast, maybe people are really into the topics," Cal had said at the time.

The course description indicated subjects like race, gender, and religion would be discussed in the context of how they related to counseling. There didn't seem to be too much enthusiasm in the room as I looked around. What was anyone going to get out of a class with such a dull atmosphere? I was about to tap Cal to ask him which student he thought would be the first to complain about being called racist, when a pair of brown loafers shuffled through the door. A tall, white, middle-aged man with stringy black hair stood at the front of the class, his collared shirt-tucked-into-corduroys outfit looking like a page out of some nightmarish professors' edition of a fashion magazine.

Cal sighed. The other Black student looked up at the ceiling in contemplation. A part of me hoped he was plotting an escape plan. I thought back to a Black film course I'd taken in college, taught by a white professor. Although the class could become uncomfortable, like during our analyses of movies about slavery, overall, I learned a lot. Maybe this new professor could teach me a thing or two about racism's impact on mental health. That is, if he could make it through the first ten minutes of class without displaying his own.

After introducing himself, the professor went through the student roster to see who was present. Finally, Brandon had a name attached to his revolutionary-inspired glasses. However, it quickly became apparent I wasn't the only one pleased to attach a name to a face.

"Brandon, Cal, Drew…Brandon, Cal, Drew."

The professor pointed at each of us in succession while audaciously repeating himself a third time.

Heads turned all across the room, snapping back to the front once they realized what just happened.

"Just keep those same seats and I'll get it right," the professor said, seemingly unaffected that we all understood he was trying not to mix up the three Black students. The smile on his face as he smoothly transitioned into going over the syllabus made the spectacle all the more unbelievable.

I knew none of the other students would speak up, so I started to raise my hand. Before it could get above my head, Cal yanked at my shirt sleeve, jerking my arm downward. I didn't understand. I glanced over at Brandon and saw him vigorously shaking his head at me, seemingly in agreement with Cal's choice to stop me from saying something.

I was steaming on the inside. What good would it do for the entire class to just let the professor get away with this? And the Multicultural Counseling professor at that!

Why should I listen to Cal anyway? I trusted him though. That same aura which gave him a sense of certainty about himself told me he somehow knew how to handle this situation better than me. So, I sat in silence for the rest of the class.

The three of us met up afterward. Cal explained the importance of protecting ourselves in a new environment. Brandon nodded along. We didn't know how the professor would respond or how our resistance would be taken throughout the counseling department. Better to be strategic and lay low until we got our footing and could address the issue in the most impactful way. This was the first hint that I would be trained in more than just counseling during my time in grad school.

TALE #2: LUCKY GUESS

BY THE TIME OUR INTERNSHIP YEAR ROLLED AROUND, BRANdon, Cal, and I had formed closer bonds with each other, a trio united by shared experiences. I often got the sense we were infiltrating this institution, unwelcome guests on a mission to simply make it out alive with diplomas in our hand.

Internships were intended to be our opportunity to put to practice the basic counseling skills and theories we had learned throughout our first year of the program. On this particular day, our cohort was meeting with faculty and some alumni who were kind enough to offer up some time and share what their internship experiences had been like.

Our trio sat among the other students, eager to begin applying everything we'd learned so far. Brandon had proven himself to be someone with a special level of insight. In the classes I had with him, he consistently offered keen observations about the client vignettes we used, expanding them into full volumes requiring deeper analysis.

Cal continued to impress. He came off as a natural in class role-plays, demonstrating newly learned counseling techniques with the deftness of a veteran quarterback who watched more game film than the rookies. I hadn't yet recognized my own talents at that point; it would take time before I learned to turn my self-scrutiny into constructive self-reflection.

At the front of the conference room, an alumna stood next to our Multicultural Counseling professor. Thankfully, I hadn't had any classes with him since, but seeing him again made me uneasy. The alumna seemed to be bantering with him, sharing laughs between exchanges rendered inaudible through the chatter from students around me. The dimming of the lights in the conference room sent a hush through the group gathered, as a PowerPoint presentation glowed alive on a screen on the front wall. The first slide explained how all students were required to do their internships at nonprofit agencies. The professor provided a brief rationale for this requirement, emphasizing the importance of getting to know the local community's culture during the course of our training. I was surprised no one could hear my, Brandon, and Cal's collective eyeroll. After a few more comments from the other faculty present, he gave the alumna the floor.

Casey, as she introduced herself, began recounting her internship experience, stroking her ponytail and switching it from shoulder to shoulder as she spoke. The nervous habit distracted me from her words until the description of her first client made my ears perk up.

"I remember it being quite difficult to form a therapeutic bond with this client," Casey said. "She would often ask me to help her out with things that had nothing to do with therapy. You know, food stamp applications, finding a bigger apartment, things like that." I had a passing thought but pushed it aside as she added onto her explanation. "Getting her to understand what therapy was for was such a challenge," she continued. "And whenever we were getting into a good groove, the session would be halted by all her questions. I spent so much time breaking down concepts to her level, progress was slow overall. Like I said, this client was quite a doozy for a novice therapist like me at the time."

Suspicion confirmed, my hand shot up. Cal and Brandon were seated across from me at the conference table, so there was no chance of stopping me this time, though their eyes showed they wanted to. Casey looked surprised, not expecting any questions to come up at this point in her story.

"Was this client Black?" I asked.

Cal and Brandon looked ready to leap over the table. The other students were as silent as I'd come to expect them to be.

"Oh, did I not mention that?" Casey responded.

"No, I think you did," I said matter-of-factly.

"Did you have a question about her background or something? Wait, did I say something wrong about—"

"No, no you're doing just fine," the Multicultural Counseling professor butted in. "Remember, everyone," he said staring straight at me. "We all engage with culture differently. What may be familiar to one therapist could be new to another and thus present a challenge in navigating."

There it was. He'd confirmed my assumption by preemptively defending her. I paused, wondering what I could say. Any critique I had to offer was already shot down by his all-encompassing "everybody's different" statement. It seemed even Casey knew she had messed up but was protected from having to own up to her judgments and her inability to meet her client's needs by the guy who'd proven himself again to be the last person who should have been teaching about culture.

Cal and Brandon's expressions rotated between I-told-you-so smugness, embarrassment, and pity for having to witness exactly what they had warned me about. I backed down into the silence that had been pushed upon me, overcome with a powerlessness I never wanted to feel again.

CHAPTER
TWO

Amir remained in the same position, his facial expres-sion flat the whole time Drew spoke. It threw Drew off. No reaction at all? For sure, given Amir's interactions with Ms. Perino, something from the stories must have been relatable.

"So? Any of that resonate with you?" Drew asked.

Finally, Amir moved, tilting his head in thought. "Sure, I guess," he strained, skepticism stretching out the last word. "I see what you're getting at with the whole Ms. Perino situation. Same stuff, different day, right? Whatever level you're at in school, this is what Black people go through."

"Yeah, you're right," Drew said. "I had a pretty naive idea that being in a program studying mental health, people would be more welcoming and accepting. You know, therapists are supposed to be so understanding of everybody. I thought faculty would at least be more aware about working to prevent racist incidents like what I experienced."

Amir's eyebrows scrunched together. "So, what's the point of your group then? Clearly, not much changes between undergrad and grad school. Are you just going to prepare us for more bad teachers? I thought this group could be a stepping stone for me, but it doesn't sound like it."

Drew was taken aback by the statement.

"Helping young, Black men prepare to become therapists is why I'm starting this group," Drew explained. "I might have got stuck in the weeds there with those school examples, but I don't want you to think that's all I'll ever talk about as a mentor. Tell me, since you were proactive in finding this 'stepping stone,' what are your reasons for wanting to join?"

"It started with my parents, I guess." Amir looked down, deep in thought. "They've worked in civil rights law for their whole careers, fighting in the courts to protect people. I'm an only child, so I think they tried extra hard to instill their values of social justice in me. Our family motto is 'freedom requires service'." He looked at Drew as if for approval. "I know it sounds heavy, but I took to it. I never knew anything else so why not? For me, working in mental health is my way of fighting for the Black community. I know from my parents how this country is still set up for us to fail. The conditions so many of our people live under make it hard for them to see a way forward, and they express that in unhealthy ways sometimes. Providing safety and making sure we can heal from the racism all around us is what drives me. I hoped your group could start me on the path toward my goals."

A pit formed in Drew's stomach. Amir's level of insight was beyond what he could have anticipated from reading his email. Yet, this wasn't what had given Drew pause. Hearing the influence Amir's parents had on his life was encouraging in its own right. Growing up in such an atmosphere, it seemed only natural to be inspired to leave a similar footprint, albeit on a different path. He slipped and sunk into the feeling in his stomach as he realized he heard echoes of an earlier version of himself in Amir's words.

He started a little as a loud ring sounded from Amir's pocket. "Sorry, can't miss this call. I'll be right back." Amir got up and went out into the hallway, leaving Drew still searching for an answer.

Drew's motivation to become a therapist had come from a different place, but essentially mirrored Amir's desire to have a liberating impact on the Black community. He'd seen a number of his friends end up in juvenile detention during his middle and high school years. Over time, he'd come to understand that the behaviors they were criminalized for deserved the attention of someone who had their well-being in mind rather than their control. He'd come into the mental health field headstrong and was met with mostly disinterest in the needs of the people he cared about most.

He managed to climb out of his internal pit and peeked his head out into the hallway to see if Amir was done with his call. He didn't see anything and couldn't hear Amir's voice coming from any direction. He peered further down, seeing Tina walking to her office while talking to a teenage girl. The tall, reedy girl slunk away toward the basketball courts before he scampered over. He didn't gauge how far he was from the wall as he tried to nonchalantly lean his shoulder against it. He scuffed the paint catching himself with his shoe.

"You okay, Drew?" Tina asked. "Don't tell me you locked yourself out of that office again." He glanced back quickly. "You look scared almost. What's up with you, man?"

"Did you see a tall guy in a black and green tracksuit walk down here? He was on his phone." Drew tried to speak at a normal pace but felt as if his words had been squeezed out of him like toothpaste from a tube.

"No," Tina said, putting her hands out as if trying to slow Drew down. "Hey, relax. What, was he calling the cops on you or something?"

"I'm not in the mood for jokes, Tina." Drew looked back and forth, hands on top of his head to try to slow his breathing. "I hope he didn't leave."

"Who?" Tina began tapping her foot impatiently.

"Amir. He's another student who wants to join my mentoring group," he explained.

Tina was behind him from the beginning when it came to starting the group. He had been rolling the idea around in his head, not sure if he had the right to call himself an expert or someone worthy of being an example for others. They only knew each other from the RCC, but Tina was a true supporter. She told him he was capable of way more than he gave himself credit for, and if he didn't start the group there would be students missing out on a great opportunity.

"Okay, so we've got an explanation," she exhaled, motioning for Drew to do the same. "I know it's been tough finding recruits, but why do you seem so frantic right now? If this Amir left without saying anything, then maybe he's not right for the group."

"That's the thing, though. I know he's right for the group. Actually, he *needs* it. If I can't talk to him again, he's going to go into this field and end up just like me." Drew almost buckled under the weight of his own words.

"What do you mean?" Tina asked. "You're sounding more and more strange, Drew. I need you to break everything down for me."

Drew thought about the parallels between his and Amir's intentions for becoming therapists. "Look, I've been doing this for a decade, but my first five years or so in the field weren't easy. I thought I could change the world, but it came crashing down on me so hard I wanted to quit. If Amir doesn't change his perspective, I'm afraid the same will happen to him."

"Well, you need to tell him that yourself." Tina pointed past Drew's shoulder, right at Amir, who was similarly leaning against the wall outside his office. "Tell him what it takes to do what you do. Give him the chance to see the kind of example you can be. You want to be a mentor? Start now."

Drew thanked her for the pep talk. He regained his composure and headed back toward Amir, hoping to redirect their discussion.

CHAPTER THREE

"Everything okay?" Drew asked as he and Amir settled back into his office.

Amir's foot bounced as it sat crossed on top of the other leg. He bit down on one side of his bottom lip. "Yeah, I'm good," he responded with a soft smile. "My parents were just checking on me," he said, wobbling his phone back and forth in his hand. "You know how it is."

"You seem pretty tight with them," Drew said. "The way their careers have inspired you and everything. When you described your drive for this work, it reminded me a lot of myself in my early days as a therapist." He scratched at the stubble gathering on his chin as he figured out how to get to his point.

"Oh, yeah?" Amir asked in a challenging tone. "Look, I didn't mean to be rude when I called your group a 'stepping stone,' but you don't have to give me the whole 'you're a younger me' speech to get me to join. I'm still interested."

Drew shrugged off the small slight. "I'm glad to hear that." He didn't know if the relief in his words was believable. Sure, he was pleased the mentor group still sounded appealing enough for Amir's taste, but he needed to let him know about his reservations. "I think you'll be a great fit for the group as long as you're careful about why you want to get into this field."

"What are you talking about?" Amir asked, eyebrows furrowed.

"It's only fair for you to know about the challenges you'll face as a therapist. I'd prove myself to be a bad mentor if I didn't warn you. For the first half of my career, things didn't go as I anticipated. I had lots of big hopes and dreams for my life as a therapist and how I'd be able to help people. Specifically, our people." As he spoke, he was transported back to those early days. He recalled being filled with confident energy, none the wiser of what was to come. "Like you, it was important for me to use my skills in service to the Black community given the harsh realities we have to face in this country."

"So, what happened? You already told me what it was like for you in grad school, so I'm guessing similar things happened as you got into the field." Amir's voice was not as critical, but he clearly needed to know where Drew was going with all this.

Amir's simple question spurred reflections of a complex time. Drew felt backed into a corner. "Hey, why don't we walk and talk for a bit," he said, shooting up from his desk and grabbing his cardigan from the chair. "It's getting a little stuffy in here, don't you think?"

Amir had no clue what Drew was up to, but trailed behind him out the door, following his instruction to leave the deadbolt pushed out in order to prop the door open.

They made a left down the hallway past Tina's office. "I figured we could use a change of scenery while we talk some more."

Before they got to the double doors of the gymnasium, the sound of rubber bouncing and sneakers squeaking against hardwood echoed toward them. Drew had barely pried the right door open when a basketball whizzed between their heads, slamming into the wall behind them.

"I got it!" Amir grabbed the ball and dribbled it through his legs a few times before tossing it underhand to the young boy standing beneath the basket in front of him.

"Sorry! I need to keep working on catching passes," the boy said with a toothy grin. He rejoined the half-court game happening on his side of the court, while down on the other end a game of Knockout was heating up. Tina had just eliminated the lanky teenager she was speaking to earlier to rambunctious screams from onlooking kids.

Drew led Amir over to the stands, where a few kids sat on the front bench waiting for their turns in the next round of either game taking place. The rest of the stands were empty, so the pair took a seat about three-quarters of the way up. "The kids here love playing against the Youth Program Director," Drew said, pointing to Tina. Amir chuckled as the court exploded with another cheer; one more kid had been eliminated. "Sometimes after a difficult session I like to come over here for a bit just to soak up some of the positive energy."

"Has our talk brought you down that much? My bad," Amir said.

"No, it's not that. I'm trying to figure out the best way to explain what I mean about the challenges you're going to face, and I think another story might help. What do you see out there?" Drew asked, motioning to the court.

"Kids having fun. Not a worry in the world."

"You think so? Sure, they all look ecstatic out there right now. Can you pick out the kids who are having trouble in school? Or the ones whose parents fight every night?"

"No, I don't think it's that easy to tell. Some kids hide it well, or maybe they're just able to have fun for a little bit when they're not focused on the bad stuff."

"Right. Just below the surface is a world we could never imagine. These kids try to make their way through it every day. And sometimes they overcome a struggle only to see their success taken away at the last minute."

TALE #3: "A" FOR EFFORT

I NEVER LIKED ATTENDING THESE MEETINGS. THE NONPROFIT I worked for stressed how important it was for us to maintain a positive relationship with the school system but had no idea the endurance required. Because I was an outsider to the school district and all the internal dynamics that came with it, my input was never taken seriously by school staff.

I slapped on another not quite sticky enough name tag as I entered the school conference room, hoping this meeting would go smoothly. Everyone gathered was there for a shared purpose, to review and update Elliott Nettles' Individualized Education Plan, or IEP, but that didn't guarantee not having issues. The school psychologist and eighth-grade teacher looked at me as if a bad smell had entered the room, though the reading and writing specialist sitting between them seemed less perturbed. Before I had a chance to break the tension, the true source of their upset trailed in behind me.

A sharply dressed man led Elliott and his mom into the conference room, introducing himself as their educational attorney. I was the one who initially recommended that Ms. Nettles contact an educational attorney to ensure the school's follow through, but apparently, I hadn't received the memo that she'd retained one already. The twisted faces I'd been greeted with made sense now. Families with legal representation always put schools in defense mode.

My dread for the meeting was somewhat eased knowing the family had another person on their side. I knew how much Elliott struggled academically before the IEP was implemented at the beginning of the school year. Like so many Black boys, his challenges were overlooked and dismissed as him being defiant, the same reason he was originally referred to me. The work I had done with him so far on managing impulsive behaviors and helping his mom establish family rules in the home, while useful, didn't address why the school hadn't recognized his need for support earlier.

While everyone got settled, Elliott sat across from me making one of his signature goofy faces. He scrunched one eye closed, while loudly snapping mint green gum between his teeth, trying desperately to draw attention. His mom darted her eyes sideways at him. I chuckled inside knowing she probably had a few choice words for him. Who could blame a thirteen-year-old for being a little antsy at a table full of stuffy adults gathered around to talk about him as if he weren't there?

The educational attorney stood up at the head of the table with the stern look of a CEO running a quarterly earnings meeting. "We are here today to review Elliott Nettles' IEP to ensure that the school has been following all provisions of the plan in order to provide him with the education he deserves." He signaled for the school staff to start.

The school psychologist ruffled through stacks of papers in front of her, a flurry of highlights and sticky tabs showing off a level of meticulousness I'd come to expect from previous meetings with her involving another student who was my client. She tended to speak in the form of proclamations, in my estimation her way of declaring superiority over me as the higher degree-holding mental health professional.

"Elliott's scores on the Beck Anxiety Inventory have fluctuated…a decrease in average CGAS and increase in CAFAS scores indicate…" she stated as if the weight of jargon and numbers would crush me under the table. I hoped she didn't notice my eyes glazing over. I seized the opportunity when she paused long enough to turn to the next annotated page.

"Those scores are surprising to me given the growth I've seen Elliott making in therapy," I chimed in.

Rather than directly respond to my comment, the school psychologist boasted about the school's recently secured funding that would allow them to hire more mental health support staff to provide more in-house care for students. She sat back, full to the brim with ego, extending her open palm as if granting me the stage.

The two other school staff shrunk slightly, uncomfortable with their colleague's braggadocio. Averting my eyes to Ms. Nettles, I briefly noted that it would be up to her to decide which care option would be best for her son. Ms. Nettles returned a soft smile while Elliott obliviously bopped his head to an internal beat, teasing us all with his privilege to tune out the meeting at his choosing.

"Let's move on to the child's academic performance," the attorney said.

I always became more alert at this part of IEP meetings. Grading methods were constantly changing and the emphasis on testing had become so overwhelming since I was a student that I had no clue what information would be presented. Ms. Nettles had allowed me to see some of Elliott's report cards— "Look at how they're failing my baby!" she'd say—but nothing compared to the first-hand perspective of those in the classroom with him.

The teacher exchanged looks with the reading and writing specialist, deciding who should go first. Given the go ahead, the teacher waved her braids behind her shoulder before proceeding. My stomach tightened with anticipation.

"How do you feel you've been doing in class, Elliott?" She was the first to directly address him since the meeting started. He continued bopping his head.

Ms. Nettles gently tapped Elliott's arm and repeated the question. He shrugged, his animated presence sloughing off with the drop of his shoulders. "Okay, I guess."

The teacher fumbled through her own stack of papers. She prefaced the readout of his grades with some context about Elliott's continued struggle to maintain focus in class. I held back from commenting about the accommodations the school was supposed to be providing for that very issue, figuring the attorney didn't need my help. Even as the teacher tried to add positive observations about Elliott's improved interactions with his classmates, I noticed how the shift in his presence progressed. He was no longer a bystander in the conversation, capable of living in his own world. Instead, he stared intently at his teacher, taking in every word. I didn't need to read his mind to tell he was processing each statement, figuring out how much meaning to attach to the low grades being listed out. Now even more hunched, he turned and looked up at his mom, as if to question whether she was buying any of this, if her view of him was changing.

Ms. Nettles shook her head as she heard how poorly her son was doing in math. "This is really unacceptable," she said.

"Well, I do want to show you what academic progress can look like at this point and how quickly it can happen." This faint offering came from the reading and writing specialist sitting next to the teacher. She introduced herself as Ms. Jacobs, explaining that she had only started working at the school that year and had been working closely with Elliott, who was reading and writing far below his grade level when the year started. This fact struck me as I thought about how a student could even fall behind to that extent and how it must feel for Elliott to know that his skills were not on the level of his classmates.

Ms. Jacobs's youthful exuberance shone through the darkness that had settled over the room as she displayed examples of Elliott's work over the fall semester. The last piece of paper she showed was an assignment in which Elliott had written a short speech explaining what he would do if he were principal for a day. "From not consistently writing in full sentences to writing full paragraphs arguing his point of view is amazing progress, Ms. Nettles. This means he is improving rapidly!"

Ms. Jacobs's excitement reflected on Elliott's face as he asked if he could read the speech to everyone. All the adults nodded vigorously, encouraging him to stand and read. He pushed his chair back and tapped his chest, dramatically clearing his throat. The room faded to the background as I locked onto Elliott and the words he shared with us.

"As school principal, I would immediately require that soda be served at lunch. Kids need the energy they get from soda so they can make it through the rest of the school day," he relayed with a politician's conviction.

I marveled at the witty ingenuity, wondering where this playfulness went by the time most of us reached adulthood. Chuckling, I said to Ms. Nettles that a soda company might call her up to offer her son a marketing job soon. Still, I remained puzzled about this one area of Elliott's progress and what it meant in the midst of all the other numbers and stats. My pen rolled back and forth between my fingers as I tried to tease out the possibilities of where he might go from here.

"I expect his reading and writing skills to continue growing throughout the school year," Ms. Jacobs added over the claps that had erupted for Elliott.

"He's going to be in high school next year, though," Ms. Nettles broke through the excitement. "He's only made these improvements with you, so what's going to happen if nobody in the high school cares enough to help him and he doesn't catch up?"

The prospects of this possibility swept around the room like a wave, knocking each person onto an elbow or back against their chair as the thought settled in.

I lost grip of my pen, not seeing where it fell; fear for Elliott's future clouded my focus. It was clear that a committed individual, not yet beaten down by the bureaucracy of the public school system, had found a way to connect with Elliott and help him excel like no one else before. Now, it seemed like he'd be going back to square one. I was interrupted from going deeper into my vortex of thoughts by the sound of sobbing. Across from me, Elliott and his mom embraced, holding each other together as her tears stained his shirt sleeve.

CHAPTER
FOUR

The game of Knockout finished, Tina losing in the final round to a young girl with ponytailed braids, now being hoisted onto the shoulders of one of the teenagers on the court. Tina looked up in the stands, catching a glimpse of Drew and Amir sitting there for the first time, and gave an amused shrug. As the celebration cleared, the half-court game expanded into a full court one, some of the Knockout players becoming makeshift referees.

"Whatever happened to Elliott? Did he find someone else to help him in high school?" Amir asked.

"I don't know actually. I ended up changing jobs not long after." Drew's first job had lots of ups and downs, but the issue was never the clients. The relationships he was able to build with them and some of his coworkers during his time there were invaluable. It was the pace of the work he ultimately couldn't keep up with. Often times it felt like the clients' well-being was put second to the company's financial goals, which put pressure on clinicians to do as much work as possible without regards to anything else, including their own stress.

"That must have eaten at you, not knowing how things turned out." Amir stared off into the distance, past the walls of the gym. "There wasn't much you could do to change the school from the outside, though," he stated matter-of-factly, returning his attention to Drew.

"You're right." Drew wrung his hands as he spoke. "As a therapist, you often work with clients connected to other systems: schools, housing programs, the criminal legal system. These systems have strong impacts on families, and our inability to directly influence them in most cases can make our jobs that much harder." Nothing frustrated him more than feeling useless. So much of therapy involved dealing with unpredictability and often intangible subjects, but the systems at work in his clients' lives were operated by real people in real places. He had assumed early on that their tangibility made them easier to change than the emotional realm. In reality, their concrete nature created a maze unreceptive toward any efforts to budge them in the right direction.

"You still didn't tell me how you felt about it." Amir directed his stare at Drew. "I wouldn't be able to sleep without knowing for sure what happened with Elliott."

"Truth is, you work with so many clients over time that if you worried about all of their futures like that, you really couldn't sleep," Drew replied, shaking his head in disbelief as he ran through the inestimable list of clients he'd worked with in the past ten years.

"Makes sense. Guess I'll have to learn how to compartmentalize," Amir said, a seriousness in his tone.

His words gave Drew pause. Out of his internal musings popped another client from his first job. His work with this client had been so pivotal, he knew from their first encounter he wouldn't forget it. He couldn't, even if he tried. "You bring up an important point I don't want to skip over. It reminds me of another client from that job. It was the first time a client's story really stuck with me."

Tale #4: Shook

I brushed the light flurries off my coat as I stepped into the school. Driving in the snow had slowed me down, but looking down at my watch, I saw there were still about five minutes until the time of the appointment. Getting there earlier would have given me more prep time, which I needed to calm my nerves. I was scheduled to conduct an intake with a new client at this school, and my head was swimming with all the information I needed to remember to gather. Even with the packet of intake questions I'd brought with me, I wasn't yet feeling comfortable with the whole process. This was my first job after my internship, where I had grown accustomed to having closer oversight by clinical supervisors. Sometimes they would even join us in the intake session to offer supportive guidance. The high school sophomore I just braved the icy roads for was only my third fully independent intake at that point, so the pressure to do well was intense.

"You can keep your gloves on, but you gotta send your hat and coat on through, baby." The school security guard directed me to place my belongings in a bin to be scanned, while motioning for me to walk through the adjacent metal detector.

I wasn't used to the heightened security. Some people claimed it was a reflection of increased concerns for school safety, but I knew the suburban schools I grew up attending still didn't have metal detectors, so something else had to explain it. The agency I worked for described many of its teen clients as "at-risk." This high school's website said the same about over half of its student body. Even though I didn't know about all the assumptions packed into the term "at-risk" at the time, I suspected it had something to do with why the school treated everyone entering like a potential threat. Gathering my navy-blue beanie and coat, I headed to the main office.

A kind looking, older Black woman greeted me when I entered. "What do you need, baby?" I was already self-conscious about not looking much older than even the seniors at the school. Being called "baby" for the second time in only a few minutes only added to the feeling. I knew it was supposed to be caring and not belittling though, so I let it go.

"Hi, I'm a counselor and I have an appointment with a student at twelve o'clock," I said. After showing my ID and providing the student's name, I was asked to have a seat while he was called down from the cafeteria.

I took the limited time to sift through my bag and do one last overview of the referral form that had come to our agency. The student, Vincent Davis, was referred by his mom for counseling. She was concerned he might be depressed because he'd recently become withdrawn and much quieter than usual. He was normally a high-achieving student, but his grades were beginning to slip in a few classes. Not much to go off, but that's what the intake was for.

A few minutes had passed when a stocky kid shuffled into the office, hands in his pockets and a pen hanging from his mouth like a toothpick. The secretary who greeted me shook her head at him. "You know, Vince, if you took your hands out of your pockets, you might have some room for that pen." He nodded but did not remove the pen. "Anyway, you have a visitor, dear," she said, motioning her hand toward me.

I stood to shake Vince's hand. "Hey there, I'm Drew. I came to talk to you for a bit today. Is that cool?"

Vince scanned me from my feet up, pausing slightly at the beanie on my head before finally freeing a hand to shake mine. He talked around the pen in his mouth. "Yeah, my mom told me you'd be coming."

"Alright, then. Well, I want to make sure you don't miss any class, so let's get to it," I said. We walked down to a vacant conference room toward the back of the main office. As we sat across from each other at the table, I took off my beanie and laid it down. Vince glanced at it like before, then shifted in his seat as if to keep it out of his view. I didn't think much of it; I was more concerned he would notice my nervousness.

I set the stapled intake packet in front of me, feeling more like a telemarketer preparing to harass someone for personal information than a trained therapist. Starting with the presenting problem, Vince didn't really give me much. He knew his mom was worried about him, but he said he felt fine. He acknowledged the drop in his grades, explaining that the work was just getting harder and his mom expected too much of him. He didn't endorse any depressive symptoms or any risk factors for self-harm. The rest of the intake categories, like family history and social supports, garnered little more than one sentence answers from him.

Next was the trauma assessment portion of the intake. I wasn't expecting much, given the fairly typical concerns Vince's mom had reported and his nonchalant presentation thus far. Still, nerves tightened my stomach. Asking about clients' trauma history was the most uncomfortable part of the intake for me, not because of what might be revealed necessarily, but because there was so much responsibility involved. Especially working with minors, the expectations of being a mandated reporter weighed me down with worries about how many details I needed to gather and wondering what would happen to kids' families if I made a report. Skipping the questions about trauma wasn't good practice though, so I braced myself and went forward with the assessment.

As I went down the list of traumas in the packet, Vince denied experiencing any of them: various forms of abuse, natural disasters, and accidents. He hesitated though when asked about the death of a loved one. I clarified, stating it could be a family member, friend, or anyone close to him who had died.

He muttered, more to himself than to me, "I haven't lost anyone, but I've seen death." His head dropped; eyes focused on his shoes under the table.

Curious, I asked him to be more specific.

Vince looked at me, only slightly lifting his head. His eye contact wasn't threatening. Rather, he seemed to be checking if I was ready for what he had to say. A hint of pity flashed across his face before he opened his mouth, like he was sorry I'd lost a bet I didn't even know I'd made.

"I saw a dead body once." Nothing in his tone showed the gravity of the revelation. He said it and now I was supposed to respond.

"You said a dead body?" was all I managed to get out. I heard him, but I hoped I was wrong, trying to suppress the unease rising in my stomach.

"Yeah," Vince said, eyes still locked on me.

"When did this happen?" I asked.

"About a year ago I guess," Vince replied.

"If you're comfortable, can you tell me more about it?"

Shifting his gaze away from my eyes, Vince nervously chewed on the inside of his cheek for a few seconds.

"I don't remember what day it was exactly, but it was kind of like today," he began. "It had snowed and I was walking home from school. The younger kids were throwing snowballs at each other and I didn't want to get caught in the crossfire, so I took a shortcut through an alley. I guess they don't shovel alleys or whatever so the snow was a little deeper. I just remember tripping over something and falling down. When I looked back, I saw a boot sticking up out of the snow. I tried to pick it up to see what kind of shoe it was, but that's when I realized it was still on a foot." This was the most Vince had said throughout the whole intake. It was like he was describing a movie scene. One that was all too real for him.

"I thought maybe someone fell just like I did, so I started moving the snow around," he continued. "I noticed this black tarp under the snow and pulled it back to get the rest of the snow off. That's when I saw him. This dude was just lying there. Shoes and pants, but no shirt. He had a navy-blue beanie pulled down all the way over his face with a dark red spot right on his forehead. I mean, it's kinda regular to hear shooting in my neighborhood, but I never saw anything like that before."

With trembling fingers, I slid my beanie from the table and stuffed it under my leg, now realizing why Vince had looked at it so strangely. I irrationally wished I had known it was a trauma reminder beforehand. My assumptions about this being a mild case now disproven, I feared how his story would end.

Vince explained how he ran home after seeing the body, afraid of what would happen if he stuck around. When his mom got in from work that evening, she told him she had seen police and an ambulance on the block where he'd run through the alley. He didn't say a word to her. The local TV news later confirmed what he saw, but he decided to keep the story to himself, figuring the best thing to do was just not walk down alleys anymore.

The school bell rang, signaling the end of the lunch period. Footsteps and loud voices in the hallway gave me the opportunity I was waiting for. "You've shared a lot today, Vince. How about I let you get to your next class and we can pick up next week at the same time?"

"Aight, cool," Vince said. "You gonna tell my mom about this?"

I let him know I wasn't required to, but I needed time to think about the pros and cons of doing so. He huffed with dissatisfaction and shuffled his way out of the conference room. I quietly counted to ten while cramming my papers into my bag. I was trying to stay calm and keep myself from darting past Vince and out of the office. Once I heard him exit through the office door, I dashed past the secretary, security guard, and metal detector, unaware of how much I was trying to outrun.

I left the school immediately feeling different. I couldn't put my finger on it, but something was off. It wasn't just some esoteric feeling either; the world around me looked different, like putting on a pair of prescription glasses that aren't your own. The quietness that accompanied the fresh snowfall added to the eeriness. Crunching my way over the salted parking lot to my car, Vince's words echoed through my head. I couldn't imagine how I would have felt coming across a body like that.

While waiting for my car to warm up, I thought about how to clear my mind. I needed something to at least distract me enough to make it to my next client. I scrolled through my phone, looking for some music to do the trick. Complex lyrics were too much to force my brain to analyze in the moment. Something poppy and light felt a little too happy-go-lucky. I needed high energy and words without much meaning, something I could lose myself in momentarily. One of my favorite trap rappers had just released a mixtape, and it was already in heavy rotation. I hit play on my favorite song off the project and locked in.

I pulled off onto the road, the hard bass and hypnotic melody of the song's beat drawing my head into a steady nod. I'd heard the song enough times to already know most of the lyrics to the verses. They'd seemed mindless before, the typical tales of hood life complete with guns, drugs, and money. After the session with Vince though, the words coming through the speakers took on a different meaning. A line about a drive-by shooting changed from what I previously thought of as the exaggeration that comes with building a rap persona into a concerning portrait of the cycle of trauma. In fact, I had somehow missed—despite leaving the song on repeat so often—the rapper's use of the word *trauma*. Being traumatized by his own carrying out of a violent act. That quickly, my tactic for distraction had become a hole to spiral down, unable to any longer find entertainment in the sounds of Black pain.

It was like that for weeks. Much of the music I listened to was suddenly too "real." I could hear the despair in the artists' voices more clearly than before. There was no more escapism in hearing the stories of a life I never lived. Sorrow took its place.

The rest of the day following Vince's intake was mostly a blur. By the time I got home, I was exhausted. Adding to it, being out in the wintry weather had me feeling the beginnings of a cold. I hoped some cold medicine would knock it out before it got worse and help me get uninterrupted sleep. A restful night wasn't awaiting me though.

Drifting in and out of sleep, I could feel a strange presence hanging over me. I thought it was just the effects of the medicine, as I'd experienced delirium from it before. As I accumulated more time fully asleep, the ethereal presence gradually became an image in my mind. There was no dream sequence or context, but when the image materialized more clearly, I didn't need to guess what it was. A skeleton with a beanie pulled over the skull hung over me, mirroring the prone position of my back against my bed. I startled awake, dripping sweat and breathing heavily.

How had my mind formed such a disturbing image of something I hadn't seen with my own eyes? If I was experiencing this just from hearing Vince tell his story, then I knew he was concealing the depth of his own trauma symptoms. I leaned over to turn on my lamp, dissipating the shadows crowding my body and infiltrating my psyche. The ceiling returned my gaze; blank, devoid of any answers for what I should do. A chill quivered down my spine, signaling my fear that the skeleton would reappear if I closed my eyes again. By the time the sun came up, I had managed to steal a few minutes of sleep here and there with the lamp on, but not nearly enough to feel well rested. I had to take the day off from work to try to bounce back.

The following day, my cold symptoms subsided enough to go into the office. Sleep had been hard to come by again, but I didn't want to miss my supervision meeting that morning. I entered my supervisor Tracy's office unsure of how I wanted to bring up what I'd experienced the past couple days. A part of me felt self-conscious about appearing as if my job was overwhelming me. Could it put my employment at risk to admit I was struggling?

"You look exhausted, Drew. Have you been sleeping well?" Apparently, my condition was bad enough for Tracy to notice within a few seconds.

I told her I'd been sick, which seemed to calm her suspicions for the time being.

"I'm glad you were able to make it today. I'm excited to hear how the intake went with Vincent this week." Tracy's smile was heartening. She was invested in my success as a new mental health professional and never missed a chance to note how much good I was going to do in my career. That enthusiasm made it harder to tell her I'd triggered Vince's trauma during our first session and was suffering from nightmares.

"It was good," was all I could say. In the silence that followed, I felt the thump of my heartbeat sync with the throbbing of my frigid ears. I couldn't bear to put on my beanie that morning, so I was paying the consequences.

Tracy broke the silence. "'*Good*' doesn't sound all that great," she said. "You know as your supervisor I have to stay on top of your work with your clients. Is there something you don't want to tell me?"

I hesitated, thinking of the best way to explain everything. I shook my head in frustration; there was no other way to tell it. "I—I'm having a hard time with this," I forced out. Like a river breaking through a dam, I let everything out. I detailed the intake with Vince and how I'd been feeling since, including the nightmares. By the time I finished spewing everything, I felt even more exhausted, yet relieved.

Tracy's reaction didn't match the despair I was feeling. She kept a steady expression, giving me time to say what I needed before responding. "I appreciate you being open, Drew. You gotta be careful out here. I'm sure you recall learning about vicarious trauma in school. What have you been doing to protect from that?" she asked.

I knew what vicarious trauma was but didn't think I could be experiencing it after one intake session.

"You seem to have had a pretty quick reaction to Vince's story," Tracy continued. "Sometimes there's so much of what I call, 'emotional gunk' stuck to us after being exposed to trauma that it's hard to clean it off before it leaves some stains. That's why consistent, preventive self-care is so helpful."

Admittedly, I didn't have a self-care plan. I had taken it to be unimportant because it seemed so superficial whenever we discussed it in school. Bubble baths, long walks, meditation. It sounded like picking up new hobbies was supposed to somehow make a difference in how I provided therapy. The visual my supervisor provided of "emotional gunk," however, helped me understand the necessity of developing a plan. I needed to know how to protect myself from the content I was being exposed to as well as be able to cleanse myself of it when it got stuck to me.

When I told Tracy this, she validated the superficial perception while adding an important point I still keep with me. Self-care might be a practice generally recommended for all therapists, but there are cultural aspects Black therapists have to be aware of. We exist within the same social structures as our Black clients, so we are often closer to the trauma they experience. Even though I came from a different socioeconomic background than Vince and had never seen a dead body, the constructed narratives of violence in Black communities were familiar to me. I also had to acknowledge my advantage in being able to psychologically guard myself from the violence while Vince had to continue living in an environment where he could encounter the same trauma again. And whether he was aware of it or not, we both had to live in a country where the root causes of the violence were unlikely to get the attention they needed, due to the perceptions about the people affected by it.

Tracy also helped me understand the unexpected risks of empathy. She explained how the connections forged through empathy were what allowed the doors to vicarious trauma to be opened in the first place. So, my struggle over the previous two days was oddly a sign of the quality of my therapeutic relationship with Vince after just one session. Because I'd already started experiencing the secondary stress from his trauma, I had to be sure it didn't push me away from maintaining my connection with him.

CHAPTER
FIVE

The basketball game wound down as a number of the players' parents arrived to pick them up, sapping the energy from the gym. Amir sat in silence, with his shoulders hunched.

"You alright?" Drew asked. "I know Vince's story was kinda heavy. Sorry I didn't warn you."

Suddenly, Amir got up and started walking down the stands, deftly descending the benches instead of the stairs. Drew called after him numerous times until he left the gym, not once looking back. Drew caught eyes with Tina, who gave him a look that said he shouldn't let Amir get away so easily this time. So, he bounded down the steps and across the basketball court, hoping to catch up.

As the gym door shut behind him, Drew saw Amir rounding the corner back in the direction of his office. "Amir!" he called again. He didn't want him to leave without explaining why. He jogged around the corner to find Amir walking at a normal pace down the hallway. He came up to Amir's side just before reaching his office.

"Hey, man, don't ignore me like that. Was it something I said? Tell me, so I can at least apologize." Drew felt like he was pleading more than necessary, but in reality, he was concerned.

Amir didn't respond as he passed by Drew's office. His backpack was still in there, so he couldn't have been leaving the building. Instead, he navigated the hallways toward the north wing of the RCC. All Drew could do was walk alongside him, waiting for an opportunity to figure out the problem at hand. To his surprise, they came to a stop at the entrance to the courtyard where the RCC's community garden stood. They walked outside and sat on a bench together. Rows of various fruits, vegetables, and flowers were grouped into boxes labeled with the names of the different elementary schools in the area that had planted them.

"This is where I went earlier when I got that call," Amir said. "It was my dad telling me how my mom was doing. She loves gardening, so it felt good to sit here while getting updated on her condition."

Drew was shocked to hear about this. "May I ask what it is your mom's going through?" he asked.

"The doctors are trying to narrow it down, but my dad says whatever it is, it's a result of the stress from working too hard over the years."

Realization flooded Drew's mind. Clarity was beginning to form around Amir. At first, his drive seemed idealistic, a hazard blinding his direction, but it now appeared more grounded. What the young man was preparing to carry on was deeper than a call to serve his community professionally. His family legacy was potentially fading.

"The one thing I don't get though," Amir said, his voice beginning to shake, "is why only she got sick. My dad did the same work for the same amount of time. He always said Mom was stronger than him too. It just doesn't make sense."

"Black women have a unique burden placed on them already, expected to take care of so many people and do so much without ever letting the effects of that show," Drew said.

Amir placed his head in his hands, trying to hold up the weight of his stress. He looked defeated.

"That's what I was getting at with Vince's story. We work in service to our community because we know what our people go through, but we're not always prepared for what we'll go through as a result of it. We can't compartmentalize our way through it," Drew said.

"I don't want to lose her," Amir said, lips quivering.

"You have a special bond with her. Hold onto it and never forget how special it is. The love and respect you have for her is something the outside world rarely, if ever, gives."

TALE #5: DEEP ROOTS

"YOU KNOW TODAY IS MY BIRTHDAY, NOT MY FUNERAL, right?"

I looked down at my outfit—black hoodie, black jeans, black boots—and apologized for not noticing the gloomy getup sooner. I felt bad for looking so out of place for the event. It was Grandma's eightieth birthday and I had agreed to come early to help set up decorations along with my mom.

"Well, don't just stand there at the door, Andrew," Grandma said. "You let enough cold air in and you just might be dressed for the right occasion." I shook my head with a soft smirk, taken by the fact that she could be so light-hearted just two years after Grandpa's passing. I locked the door behind me, removed my boots—revealing black socks—and walked in toward the sounds coming from the kitchen.

The last synths of one of those 80s R&B hits I knew all the words to, but could never name, faded out as I spotted Mom. An impressive mock-vibrato pulsed over the slim, brass candle holder clutched in her hand. She ended her performance with a bowed head as she gave a dramatic turn toward her new audience.

She looked up and took a quick step back. "Take whatever you want, just don't shoot!" she shouted, hands raised above her head.

"Ha. Ha. You and Grandma should put some kind of comedy routine together," I snarked before hugging her. "Don't worry, Mom, I've already been put on notice for my outfit." I gave an exaggerated frown.

"Why didn't you notice you were coming to your grandma's birthday dressed like this?" she asked.

"I don't know, I guess I was just a little distracted. There's been a lot of things on my mind," I responded.

Mom's tone softened. "Is it that job of yours?" she asked. "Ever since you started, you've had these moods that you get into. I can hear it in your voice on the phone but seeing you now I feel like there's more going on."

Grandma paused briefly while grabbing some glasses from the cabinet. "Don't tell me they've been treating my baby badly over there. Not my star therapist," she said.

Mom pursed her lips in my direction, a hand on her hip. I tried to ignore her, wanting to avoid any stress. This party was the only opportunity for relief I'd have all weekend.

"No, it's not that, Grandma," I replied, caving to my mom's insisting gesture.

"I've just been really stressed out by certain situations," I said, pushing up the sleeves on my hoodie. Sometimes leaving work felt like an escape; like the proverbial frog who has just enough awareness to realize the water surrounding it has become uncomfortably hot. Except the pot I was in was one I had to return to eight hours a day, five days a week. "Come to think of it, you both might have some insight into what's been going on at work."

Mom put the back of her hand to her forehead, pretending to faint. "Drew, you haven't asked me for help since I was wiping your butt! You must be stumped for real."

"You know we never talked about therapy in my day," Grandma added, "so I'm not sure what help I can be."

"It's not anything clinical really," I explained. "It's the way my coworkers talk about some of our clients. I feel like whenever someone is working with a Black woman, a Black mother especially, a lot of unfair judgment comes into play."

The previous week, a white female coworker of mine was doing a case presentation in our staff meeting. She was asking the team for tips on how to support her teen client when the mother did not reinforce any of the skills they had been working on. She gave the team a brief summary of the mom's history, indicating she had been through her own struggles since childhood. Before allowing the team to offer suggestions, she had closed her presentation by saying, "It's clear this mom doesn't want to do what it takes to raise her daughter, and until she steps up to the plate, I don't know what else I can do here."

As I told this story to Mom and Grandma, they looked as if someone had slapped them. "And she said this about a Black mother?" Mom asked, eyes wide. I nodded.

"How long has this coworker of yours been a mom?" Grandma followed up. When I said she wasn't a mom,

Grandma sucked her teeth and began to mutter to herself inaudibly. Although I couldn't hear what she was saying I heard the lilt in her voice change. Grandma had mastered masking her Caribbean accent decades ago, but it still crept out under certain conditions, like when she was upset.

While this coworker's statement was the most egregious one I'd heard, other comments in a similar vein were more common than I felt comfortable telling Mom and Grandma. I had managed to keep my mouth shut up to that point, but the constant barrage of insults was making it harder. The disrespect was personal. I would hate to know someone was talking about my own mother like that behind my back. "What do you guys think I can do about it without seeming like the Black guy that makes everything about race?"

"This is about race though," Mom said. "There's no way around it. Does anyone else have a problem with these comments?" There were enough Black people at my job, including my supervisor, to assume I wasn't the only one affected. In fact, I recalled a couple times when my eyes met my supervisor's with a knowing look when a similar remark was made, yet there was still no follow through.

"Yeah, but I don't think any of us know what to do, Mom," I said. "You know what it's like trying to call white people out at work. Even if you're the boss, it can backfire somehow."

"Hmph." Mom crossed her arms. "Oh, I know. Black women are the subject of so much abuse and then have to sit back and accept it for fear of being targeted even more."

The three of us made our way into the dining room to finish setting the table. It could only seat about a quarter of the people expected at the party, but Grandma needed it to look right regardless. The table was a prized possession, designed by Grandpa with the carpentry skills he learned from his father.

"It sounds to me like this girl needs to have more understanding and less judgment," Grandma said. "Why not try to figure out how they were affected by their experiences instead of blaming them for how things turned out?"

"I agree, Grandma," I said. "You're better at this therapy thing than you think. I can't force a young, white woman to empathize with Black women, though. If that were the case, a lot of things in this country would be different."

Just then, the doorbell rang.

"Must be your father," Mom said. "Let's hope he picked up the right drinks. Even with a list, he gets carried away sometimes." She strolled toward the front door, leaving Grandma and me to place the final plates and glasses.

"Come take a look at this over here," Grandma said, leading me over to the adjacent den. She pointed above the forest green couch centered on the far wall to a painting I'd seen since my childhood. It was a picture of two towering peaks, keeping watch over a town nestled below among dense green foliage and hugged by the bluest of water at its shores. These were the twin Pitons of St. Lucia.

"Leaving my home to come here was not easy." Her accent was back, as stories of home also allowed it to flourish in the open. I loved hearing her childhood stories about growing up on the small island, my West Indian heritage being a source of great pride.

"Yes, and look at what you accomplished," I said, taking in our surroundings. This house had raised children and cared for grandchildren for so long, love was baked into its walls. Admiration didn't even begin to describe how I felt about my grandparents' perseverance. I reminded Grandma of this as often as I could.

"Mmm," Grandma nodded slowly. "Even so, I've always wondered if we could have made it through what the others did," she said, blinking through a series of thoughts. "You know when we came to this city there were many others heading up here too. Not from the islands, but from the Southern United States."

I nodded, trying to follow her reference to the Great Migration. She didn't talk about her actual immigration experience much.

"When we got here some of our neighbors told us about the horrible conditions they fled from," she continued. "No jobs and no hope. Unthinkable violence for going against even the smallest of social rules that sound like fiction now. You see, we made our decision to come to this city for opportunity, whereas others ran here for safety. And when they got here, guess what?"

"There was still racism up North. The conditions weren't necessarily better, just different." Talking to someone who lived the history I'd only read about made me feel closer to the experiences.

"That's right," she said. "If there's anything Black people know, it's that as much as things change, they stay the same."

I couldn't argue with that. "I think I'm following you, Grandma. But how does this history help with what I'm dealing with at work?"

"What I mean is, our histories stay with us. Regardless what path any specific family took, Black families have been running and searching for safety in some way for centuries. What do you think that could look like after a few generations?"

Grandma's insight got me thinking. My coworker had tunnel vision, limiting the context of her client's mom's behavior only to her personal history, creating an image in which she had "failed" to become a successful parent. "Man, thanks for the advice, Grandma. I'll make sure to mention your name when I get fired for speaking up."

"Don't expect to move back with us after you get fired, now." A hand clapped my right shoulder. I turned to see my dad laughing, clearly not needing anyone to validate his humor. I gave him a hug once he recovered from his own joke.

"What's going on, Dad?"

"I just brought by everything your mom asked me to get," he replied.

"With some bottles of liquor I definitely did not put on that list!" Mom projected from the kitchen.

Dad gave the exaggerated shrug he was prone to whenever he conceded to Mom being right. "This is supposed to be a celebration, right? I think you two need the first drinks," he said, looking back and forth between Grandma and me. "Your mom told me y'all were having a deep discussion over here. Why'd you have to go and get your grandma all stressed out on her birthday?"

I filled Dad in on where the conversation stemmed from. I asked him his perspective, hoping he'd have some helpful thoughts. He let out a deep breath, resting his hands in his pockets as he thought.

"See, guys in your generation try to hide behind hashtags about protecting Black women to avoid the real work of it." I cringed whenever Dad referenced "my generation," but he had a good point this time. Although I appreciated how my age group strived to make society better, we had a knack for oversimplifying complex issues into easily repeatable phrases without focusing on the work needed to make them a reality.

"I get it. There are no clear steps for me to take in this situation," I said.

"I don't think it's about having some rigid protocol to follow," Dad explained. "Think more about the purpose. At your job, you're all supposed to be helping people with their mental health in some way. If this coworker of yours has such a biased opinion about this mom, then she can't work effectively with her, meaning the family won't get the help they need. So, protecting this mom means making sure she and her daughter get the best care they can from someone who can best provide it."

"Whew, that dad of yours is pretty sharp," Grandma remarked. "You could have saved a lot of time just talking to him."

Combining Dad's and Grandma's advice created a clearer picture in my mind. With a better contextual understanding of her clients' lives, and some much-needed humility, my coworker could be better equipped to meet their needs. Or not. Getting anything through to her would first require her realizing the harm she was do-ing by criticizing the mom in such a way. That first step seemed like a leap across a canyon.

"Thanks for the input, everybody," I said, leaning back to peer through the dining room to the kitchen where Mom was sorting out the drinks. "I'm going to bring this up to my supervisor and figure out the best way to address the issue."

Another ring at the doorbell made the three of us in the den turn. Dad looked down at his watch. "Almost showtime! Drew, go get the door, and Ma, go upstairs so you can change into your birthday outfit."

I patted down my hoodie as I approached the front door, wishing it were a nice button-down shirt, or at least a more festive color. I swung open the door to a welcome scene: my aunt and uncle, swinging my little cousin be-tween their arms up onto the porch, followed by a couple of Grandma's friends who I recognized from the occa-sional weekends I'd brought her to the local senior center. Hugs and kisses went around as they all streamed into the house. Gradually, more guests arrived, filling the space with a buzz of excitement.

I maneuvered around the house, observing all the interactions between family, friends, and those who were meeting for the first time. Drinks flowed and conversation filled the air. When the time came, Mom started up the playlist again, this time an unfamiliar 50s-sounding tune, as we all looked toward the staircase and cheered, mark-ing Grandma's grand entrance with a well-earned show of love.

CHAPTER
SIX

"How was that supposed to help me?" Amir asked. Dusk settled around him and Drew, not yet dark enough to trigger any of the outdoor lamps. Amir's face was cast in shadows as he turned. "My mom is probably dying and you decide to tell me how I'm going to have to put up with colleagues putting down Black women?"

Drew was embarrassed. Why hadn't he considered the anticipatory grief Amir must have been experiencing? "Since you're so close with your mom, I figured you should know the environments you might find yourself in," he explained, trying to recover. "You may need to pick your battles in order to make it through."

"Isn't that part of our fight, though?" Amir countered. "The odds are against us already, so ignoring disrespect will only make it worse."

"I thought the same thing at one point. Trying to go it alone was my mistake from early on," Drew explained. Despite making friends with some coworkers, he felt disconnected from most of the people around him, like the things he cared about weren't important to anybody else.

"I'm not you!" Amir shouted, his hands tensing like claws. "You've been telling me all of these cautionary tales so I don't make the same mistakes as you." A sly smirk curled the corner of his mouth as he shook his head. "It's *you* at the center of all your stories, but you try to make everyone else seem like the problem."

Drew sat frozen. He didn't expect such a display of anger from Amir. "Yes, it has been all about me, Amir. That's the point." The bite of his tone lingered on his tongue. "If you don't listen and take this seriously, you will become me, despite your conviction that we're nothing alike. You don't know what it's like to be committed to a profession that makes no room for you and lets you down so much that you want to quit." The garden, the bench, and Amir disappeared around him as he sunk into the pit of memories from his early career. As isolated as he felt back then, Amir's dismissiveness re-opened the wound. Again, he couldn't get someone to see his point of view. "I'm trying to protect you!" The proclamation came from deep inside.

"Trust me, you're no savior," Amir rebutted.

Still halfway in the pit of his past, a small spark lit up Drew's mind. "I don't want to be a savior. And neither should you."

Amir shot him a dirty look before getting up to go back inside.

"Wait!" Drew grabbed Amir's arm. "Hear me out." He mentally scrolled through other stories he could tell. "There was this time when…um, well, it was actually a friend who told me…" He had nothing. He was trying to stall, but Amir clearly wasn't going to give him more time.

Amir stood with his arms crossed and head cocked to the side. "You out of stories, finally?"

"No," he lied. "It's just…okay, so there were two guys," Drew stammered.

"Please stop," Amir snapped. "You're embarrassing yourself now."

Amir was at the end of his rope, so Drew had to come up with something. *Here goes nothing*, he thought.

Tale #6: Two Sides of a Worthless Coin

The elevator took so long to reach the third floor, he later wondered if it was trying to warn him about what he was walking into. The suite was not as bustling as he expected a successful group private practice to be. Sure, it was an office meant for therapy, but the hush over the simply decorated space bordered on unsettling. He checked the emailed acceptance letter on his phone again to make sure he was in the right place. Confirming, he headed back toward the sound of typing coming from an office with its door slightly cracked open.

A blonde woman introduced herself as the practice owner and supervisor. "Hi, Harold! We're so glad you decided to join us! Diversity is our company's top value, and we can't wait to see how you will contribute to our team." She sounded like a recording, her measured cadence ensuring she emphasized the right words. She had clearly been practicing her lines.

Harold sat across from the supervisor, listening to her explain the struggles the company had been experiencing with certain clients who just weren't seeing the improvements others were making. She said all the effort in the world wouldn't make a difference because these clients were so resistant to bonding with their therapists. Her explanation of the problem was vague, so he asked her to elaborate.

She momentarily looked up and to the side, like she was trying to remember another line. "We've been in desperate need of someone who's an intentionally competent connector with relevant cultural touchpoints." The words were like puzzle pieces being forced together.

"You mean you need a Black guy to work with your Black clients?" Harold asked. "You could have at least put it in the job description."

Her head whipped back so fast, he thought she was dodging an unseen fly in the room. Her head came back down, strands of blond hair crisscrossing over a gaping smile plastered on her face as she let out a stilted laugh. The hollow sound and her stiff movements made her resemble a marionette. "You are so funny! I'll let our recruiters know to do that next time. No, I'm joking. That would be so bad, right?"

"Um. Yeah." He blinked hard, as if trying to reset the scene in front of him. He sat rigidly in his chair, bracing himself for another awkward interaction.

She readjusted her hair behind her shoulders. She let him know he wouldn't meet his first client until the next day, so the rest of his time in the office that day would be spent shadowing another therapist's sessions. Harold didn't bother to ask why he needed to shadow when his résumé had clearly stated he had ten years of clinical practice under his belt. He hadn't seen anyone else in the suite when he came in, so he asked where to go to meet the other therapist.

"Head over to the office next to the coffee maker," she instructed. "You'll know her when you see her."

He began to circle around the suite until he spotted the coffee maker sitting on a table in the corner. As he got closer, he saw four packs of Kenyan coffee grounds resting next to it, all unopened. The way they were lined up looked like an intentional display. In the small garbage can under the table, he spotted a grocery store bag with a partially crumbled receipt laying on top of it. It wasn't much of a dumpster dive, so he let his curiosity guide his hand to the receipt. Pulling it out to read, his suspicion was confirmed. The coffee grounds had just been purchased that morning. He tore the receipt in multiple pieces and sprinkled them back in the trash.

When he rounded the door frame into the adjacent office, he was stunned by the sight before him. A deep brown-skinned woman with a crown of locs spiraled neatly on top of her head made eye contact with him. "Thank God! So, you bought the coffee?" Harold asked. "I thought it was some kind of welcoming gift for me since, well, you know. I didn't expect to see you," he stammered.

"Oh, no, that wasn't me," she said. "You were right. They bought Tanzanian coffee when I started."

"Wait, from the way my meeting with the supervisor just went, I thought I was the only, maybe even the first, Black person working here," he said.

"There's never two of us here for long, so my time might be running out," she said. "Regardless, every time I change my hair, she acts like she's never met me before, so who knows. Maybe she actually forgot about me." She didn't sound hurt, but her body language said otherwise. "If she remembered I existed, she might have asked if we were related or something. So, consider yourself lucky."

Harold struggled to make sense of everything he'd experienced so far that morning. "How long have you worked here?"

"Too long." She shook her head.

"Why have you stayed if it's so bad?"

"They're guilty as hell, so they pay more than a lot of other places just to attract diversity hires."

Something felt off. "The money can't be worth your dignity though. I was just told I'm basically here to 'save' the Black clients."

She nodded in a knowing way, followed by a shrug. "I mean, who else is going to do it if not us? With the way she just talked to you, imagine what she's like with Black people actually looking for help."

His head spun. He tried to think of a rebuttal even though he knew she was right to some extent. He hated the idea of leaving Black people out there at the whim of people who didn't care about them, but the resulting burden of caring for the community was a heavy responsibility.

The rest of the afternoon passed by in a blur. Very little content from the therapy sessions Harold shadowed stuck with him. He recalled a couple of the clients being pleased that another Black therapist was joining the practice, but not much else could make it through the whirl-wind of emotions whipping around his head. Leaving the office, all he could think about was getting a strong drink and retiring to bed early.

He came back the next day feeling tense. Between his interactions with the supervisor and his sole Black co-worker, he wasn't sure he should even be walking back into the suite. As the elevator dinged at the third floor, the doors slid open to the supervisor's face, eyes wide and teeth bared, not so much a smile as an exhibition of their gleaming whiteness. He jumped back, startled.

"Good morning, Harry! I'm so excited for today! Your first client's going to arrive in about thirty minutes, so let's go talk about the case for a bit."

He responded with a quiet greeting and followed alongside her back to her office.

She continued as they sat down. "You know, when I was leaving the office yesterday evening, a woman got on the elevator who resembled you so much. Do you have any siblings?"

He stared blankly. "You think I have a sister who just so happens to work in the same building, on the same floor as me and I just hadn't brought it up yet?"

She returned his blank stare. "I'll take that as a 'no'." She turned to her computer, clicking around for a few minutes with her back to him, pausing as two sheets of paper slid out of her printer.

She turned back and handed him a copy of his client's referral form for him to follow along as she explained the case. The client was a ten-year-old boy who was reported-ly experiencing depressive symptoms. He did not want to play with his friends as much and was often caught sleeping in class. The boy's mom didn't know what to do to help him. She said she loved her son so much and just wanted his old self to come back.

The supervisor asked if Harold had any initial ideas about how he would approach the case. He told her CBT was the modality he felt most comfortable using.

"Amazing! I can't wait to see all the progress this kiddo makes!"

In the back of his mind, he wondered whether she knew CBT stood for Cognitive Behavioral Therapy and not Cultural Black Teachings. What did she expect him to do differently with this client? She probably thought somehow their shared Blackness would moonwalk them down the path toward healing.

When the client and his mom finally arrived, Harold was more than happy to escape from the supervisor. The kid's mom looked spaced out until he got closer; then her face beamed. "Thank God you're Black! The Lord has answered my prayers. We've been needing you for so long." She ran down a list of all the ways her son needed help and how only a Black man could get the job done. "His absent father, his bad grades, he has no male role models, his attitude, he has no men to guide him, he's disrespectful, he has abandonment issues from his father leaving…"

He didn't yet know why the referral hadn't mentioned the extra concerns, but the mom's focus was clear. "Look, I get it. Really, I do," he said. "I know the stats and everything. I mean, heck, I've lived them. My dad wasn't around either. But don't you think this is a little weird?

Given the mild nature of your son's actual symptoms, he probably won't need to be in therapy that long. So, you want me to form a tight bond with your son, and then after, I don't know, maybe half a year just bounce? Do I need to point out the irony here?"

"What are you trying to say?" the mom asked, exasperation coloring her voice.

"What I'm saying is, I'm a therapist. It's fine if your son sees me as someone to look up to, but I'm here to help him, not raise him."

A reflex deep within him activated after uttering those words. He flinched in anticipation of a slap, since that's exactly what his own mother would have given him for speaking so freely. No attack came, though. The mom simply gathered her things and pulled her son after her as they headed for the door. The boy looked back over his shoulder, dissatisfaction dragging his face down into a melting frown. His eyes gleamed with what seemed like tears ready to fall, until they turned into a mischievous glint and he stuck his tongue out before disappearing into the elevator.

After Harold relayed the debacle to the supervisor, he was fired.

<hr>

One Week Later

"Welcome, Gerald! Diversity is so valuable to us. You're going to be such a trailblazer, showing us how it's done." The supervisor explained the troubles therapists at the practice were having connecting with certain clients.

She said some cases just felt impossible with so much resistance to the process.

Gerald hung on to her every word, nodding along in agreement. "I understand. It must be so hard getting buy-in from your Black clients. But, with me they won't need to explain anything in session. I get it because I have shared cultural touchpoints with them. I move with cultural intentionality in my work, beyond cultural competency, so I can connect on a deeper level."

If she smiled any wider, her face would split. "OMG, Gerry! You're exactly what we've been waiting for," she overflowed, squeezing out each syllable.

"I'm glad to be here," he smiled back. "Whatever I need to do to make this place better for Black clients, I'm ready. A little extra effort never hurts."

The supervisor told him there was a new hire who was fired after only two days because he didn't have Gerald's positive attitude. She then explained he wouldn't be meeting his first client until tomorrow, so he'd be shadowing another therapist for the rest of the day. "You'll know her when you see her," was the only description given as he was pointed toward his new colleague's office.

On his way over, he was drawn to the nearby coffee maker, as the packaging for Kenyan coffee caught his eye. He opened the bag and took a whiff. The aroma hugged his body, transporting him back to the trip he'd taken to Kenya a few years ago. As he began to brew a cup for himself, he heard the click of heels approaching behind him. He turned to see a deep brown-skinned woman with a crown of locs spiraled neatly on top of her head looking at him with an eyebrow raised.

"You're actually drinking that? You know they only buy that stuff when they hire a Black person," she said.

"This 'stuff'," Gerald replied defensively, "is some of the best coffee in the world. I see it as a testament of this clinic's commitment to inclusion that they would stock the office according to the demographics of the folks working here."

"That's an…optimistic way of looking at it," she said with disbelieving eyes rolling toward the ceiling.

"Why are you so easily displeased, Queen?"

She rubbed her temples. "Please, miss me with all that Hotep stuff."

He laughed in a self-assured manner. "That's an odd way to respond to respect. Why are you still working here if this place is so terrible?" He slowly looked her outfit up and down as he hissed, "It can't be the money."

She glared back at him, biting her lips closed. After a deep breath, she proceeded to give him a rundown of her afternoon schedule and the sessions he would be able to sit in on. He asked her what culturally-based interventions she used with her Black clients.

"There's no magic spell in my toolbox. I listen to my clients and meet them where they are, offering support in the ways that work best for them."

Except, that didn't work best for Gerald. He tried to sit quietly while shadowing one of his new colleague's sessions. Shadows were supposed to stay out of the way, but he couldn't remain in the background. He thought she was completely ignoring the cultural contexts of the client's problem. When she again asked about how the client was doing with practicing a coping skill, he interrupted.

"Coping won't help! This is a young Black man you're talking to. Telling him to cope is telling him to accept his position in society as a second-class citizen. Every 'tool' you give him to use is just another weight on his back, holding him down. Shame on you, sista!" He stormed out of the session before either could respond.

The next day, the supervisor swiftly pulled Gerald into her office. "I heard all about your little stunt yesterday, Gerry."

He straightened his back, ready to be on defense.

"You. Are. Amazing! A star!" The supervisor's face lit up. "Your little friend across the hall there tried to file a complaint about you, but when I heard all the details, I stopped her in her tracks. What you did in that session yesterday is exactly what I've been looking for."

Smug satisfaction dripped from Gerald's face. "Thank you. I'm not here to offer anything less." He then eagerly received the referral form for his first client, ready to continue to impress. Apparently, the young client and his mom were severely disrespected by the fired therapist they met the previous week and were ready to start on a new path.

Upon meeting the family, Gerald immediately apologized for the poor experience they had the last time.

"Oh, it's not your fault," the mom said. "Some people just can't live up to the task, and instead of admitting it, choose to lash out."

"Sounds like you'd be a great therapist yourself," Gerald said. He went on to describe his culture-centered approach to treatment to the mother. She nodded along in excitement, urging him to please help her son become the King he was meant to be.

The session had barely started before it was over, the child running out of the room after only a short time. "Mommy, he's scary!" the boy wailed, a trail of incense wafting out of the room behind him.

"What did you do to him?" the mother demanded of Gerald.

"It seems your son is too sensitive to confront the realities of being a young Black man in this country," he replied. "If he can't keep it together for more than ten minutes, I don't know if there's much I can do for him."

The mom gave a sharp stare before again gathering her things and dragging her son out of the building.

CHAPTER
SEVEN

"THIS IS RIDICULOUS," AMIR MUTTERED UNDER HIS BREATH, rushing back inside before Drew could stop him.

Drew kicked the bench. What was he thinking? His impromptu story had failed miserably. His last-ditch effort at showing Amir the pitfalls of his current path ended up pushing the young student further away than he could've imagined.

Inside, Amir's long, quick strides carried him down the hallway. "This whole time you've really seen me as some kind of idiot waiting to be taken advantage of or willing to sell myself out?" he snapped over his shoulder.

"No, I don't think those things at all," Drew replied. "But whether we think of ourselves as saviors or others ask us to be, the results aren't good." His words were as effective as pebbles thrown at a tank. There was no point in trying to explain anymore.

Drew arrived at his office just as Amir was turning out the door with his backpack slung on his shoulder. They met face to face. "I'm done with this," Amir said with cold, unmoving eyes.

"I'm sorry, Amir. I didn't mean to upset you like this." Drew stood tensely, more than slightly afraid Amir would push right through him.

Amir simply shook his head. "I'm not upset. I'm relieved actually now that I think about it. No wonder you haven't found anyone for your little group yet. You've proven yourself to be a bad mentor, one who's looking for excuses around every corner. Who would want that?" He scoffed as if disgusted at the sight of Drew. "I'm out of here."

Drew slouched out of his way, this time making no effort to stop Amir from marching out of the building.

"One thing you're right about," Amir said, glancing over his shoulder. "I don't want to be anything like you. Not a counselor, not anything."

The sting hit Drew in the center of his chest, emptying out all sense of hope. Out of ideas for what to do, he watched his best chance at starting the mentor group barrel out the front doors.

CHAPTER
EIGHT

The words replayed again and again on Drew's drive home. They hurt. Not because they were mean, but because they were true. Who would want to follow in the steps of or take any advice from someone hurling a barrage of cautionary tales at them? He blamed himself for being so easily triggered by Amir's career motivations. He thought he was past the trauma of his early experiences in the field, but clearly the effects lingered.

He didn't try reaching out to Amir immediately. There was too much to sift through. He couldn't make sense of why he'd been so relentless about trying to prove his point instead of just accepting his first group member and taking things from there. The deadline to start the program was only getting closer, so he had to act.

Drew began Thursday morning with the first of several pleas. He only had Amir's email address, so he frantically typed a message which read in part:

> I apologize for how things went yesterday. I'm sure you probably regret coming to see me. You have to believe that I didn't intend to offend you. I know this is a long shot, but if you're up for it I want to talk again. I'll leave my number below so you can call or text me if that works better for you.

He had a full schedule of clients to meet with virtually that day. Normally, he closed all other programs and browser tabs while in session, but he couldn't resist keeping his email open, doing his best to sneak glances at his notifications while attending to what his clients were saying. His only success was in not getting caught looking. Other than that, he failed at retaining much content from his sessions, relying on the therapist cheat code he learned early on in grad school: repeat the last sentence or phrase you heard from the client as a question, and ask for them to explain in more detail.

"That was the lowest point of your week? Tell me more about that."

"You can't stand sitting in traffic? Tell me more about that."

None of Drew's clients made much progress, and neither did he in getting a response from Amir.

His phone had buzzed once, with a text from Tina.

Hey, I saw that kid Amir storm out yesterday. Everything good?

Everything was not good. He put his phone on silent for the rest of the night.

Friday mirrored the day before. The words of Drew's clients drifted past him as he grew even more distracted, waiting for a reply from Amir. He was happier than usual when his last two clients of the day canceled their sessions. Now he had time to craft a follow up message to Amir.

Okay, maybe I was being too forward asking you to talk again so soon... What do I need to do to change things here? Trust is never easy to build, I know... Look, this is an opportunity we'll both miss out on if nothing gets fixed...

The whole thing read like a beggar's monologue to an ex that was already too far gone. No sense of shame or embarrassment came along to stop Drew from sending it. For the rest of the night, he sat in his apartment, TV on in the background, staring at his laptop anxiously waiting. He grabbed a beer from the fridge to calm his nerves. His garbage can was the only thing keeping track of how many drinks he had before he dozed off on the couch. No ping, ring, or buzz sounded to disrupt his sleep.

On Saturday, the feeling of his brain pulsing woke Drew up. His laptop sat on the cushion next to him, only a sliver of energy left on the battery icon. No new emails. On his phone, two more texts from Tina. He couldn't keep his eyes on the glaring screen long enough to type a response. He'd kept the blinds open overnight, the sunlight intensifying his hangover with a relentless burn.

As he shifted to sit up on the couch, his foot knocked the last empty beer bottle off the coffee table, sending it rolling over to the bookshelf in the corner of his living room. Drew groaned as he got up, holding a hand to his head. Bending over to pick up the bottle, his eyes met the bottom shelf. He glanced at the collection of video games he kept there, collecting dust since work didn't allow much time for them anymore. One in particular stood out; *Finder's Keeper* was the title. Pulling the case out slightly to look at the cover, images of jumping across platforms, fighting off robbers, and car chases flashed through his memory. He'd played the game non-stop when it first came out but hadn't thought much about it since.

Drew shuffled his way to the kitchen to throw away the beer bottle and start gathering himself when he suddenly remembered why that game out of all the others caught his eye. He inched back to the shelf and grabbed the game, inspecting the cover again. There it was in the bottom corner, the symbol on the pin on Amir's backpack: the head of a yak with lightning bolts protruding where the horns should be. It was the game developer's logo. Mannyaac Games, it read underneath. With his mind coming back into focus through the lingering haze, Drew recalled why this game was so important to him.

He spent the morning into the early afternoon rummaging through what shouldn't have been so many potential hiding spots in a one-bedroom apartment. He searched between books on the shelf, in the closet, and in his desk drawers. Nothing. Where could it have gone? He wouldn't have thrown away such a special possession.

Drew spun around, hands clasped on top of his head, aimless and losing hope. As he stopped, his gaze settled on a framed graduation photo of himself, Brandon, and Cal that he kept over his work desk. *There!* Taking the blown-up photo off the wall, he opened up the back of the frame, revealing what he'd been looking for. Pressed against the back of the photo was a magazine. Drew thumbed through the pages, looking for a particular article. He read it over, nodding at each passing paragraph, reassuring himself that the words were capable of accomplishing what he believed they could. Smiling to himself, he tucked the magazine away in his messenger bag.

The next few days crawled by, making Drew's anticipation grow to the point of annoyance. Eventually, his Wednesday evening back at the RCC arrived. This time he was ready.

It only took one hard pull to open his office door, surely a positive sign, Drew thought to himself as he entered. Even as he'd walked up to the community center that afternoon, the building's facade seemed to showcase a unique character where he previously only saw flaws. After a week of turmoil turned self-reflection, he was looking at things through a different lens.

"Oh, so you're alive?" Tina's voice surprised him. She stood at his door with her arms crossed, waiting for an answer.

"Hey, Tina. Sorry about this weekend," he said with hunched shoulders.

"This weekend? You let a whole week go by without responding to any of my texts! Don't worry, I didn't stress about it. I've got enough to manage around here as it is. I hope you got yourself together, though."

"I'm sorry. Really, I am. There was a lot going on for me." He felt bad about not answering Tina. Her support probably would have been better than processing everything alone. "When I left out of here last week, I felt defeated. I didn't want to talk to anybody about what happened because there was nothing to say. Not until I regained my dignity and got Amir to come back." It wasn't clear the apology was fully accepted, but Tina appeared less upset.

"So, you patched everything up with Amir?" she asked.

"No, I haven't spoken to him since last week. He didn't respond to any of my emails, understandably."

"Emails, like plural? You're really chasing this kid, huh?"

"I'm not proud of my methods either. Although, I think I found something that will work," he said, patting his messenger bag. He unzipped it to show Tina the magazine when a tall, hooded figure peaked in behind her.

"Hey, Lo!" Drew said with a smile on his face. "Can you give me and Ms. Tina a minute before you and I check-in?"

"Oh no, don't let me get in your guys' way," Tina stated. "I wouldn't want this young man to feel ignored or anything." She raised her eyebrows at Drew and politely patted Lo on the shoulder as she exited the office. Drew sighed, hoping things would smooth over between them. He was still in a good mood though, so he redirected his focus to where it was currently needed.

"Have a seat, Lo. What's been going on?" Drew gestured to the green chair.

Lo slid with his back against the wall from the door frame into the office but did not sit down. He kept his eyes closed; hands stuffed in his hoodie pocket.

Drew closed the door with his foot and reached over the desk to place his bag on the office chair. Then, leaning back, he sat lightly against the desk while staying at eye-level with Lo. "I know this building's old, man, but I don't think you need to hold the wall up like that." No quick response to the dad joke from Lo or even an acknowledgment that he'd heard it. "Okay. At least I can say I tried. Well, what can you tell me about what's happened over the last week? Any updates on football?"

Lo huffed, the first sign of any attention coming from him. "Football's going just fine, but my girl left me thanks to you!" His eyes shot open at the last word, digging deep into Drew's own.

"Wait a minute, what do you mean?" Drew made sure not to tell any of his clients what to do, especially the teens who were constantly seeking reinforcement around their decision-making. Even if they directly asked him for advice, he knew better than to give in. Reactions like Lo's were often the result.

"When I told her I needed to find more 'balance' between her and football, she said she'd make it easier by eliminating one of the options." Lo kept his glare locked on Drew.

Drew calmy nodded along, listening for what lay underneath his anger. "Your relationship was really important and losing it makes keeping your spot on the team not seem worth it. And you've played football most of your life, but having a girlfriend was a new experience. Sounds like a tough loss to deal with." He was being more directive in labeling Lo's thoughts and feelings than he usually liked to be, but he wanted to sideline the blaming and get to the core of the issue.

Lo sucked his teeth. "Yeah, I guess," he mumbled in reluctant agreement.

They both settled into their respective seats and continued discussing the breakup. Drew focused on the aspects of loss in order to explain how there was a kind of grieving process Lo would have to go through. This was important to establish before the younger mind hopped to solutions for getting his girl back or choosing to just move on without processing his feelings. Lo seemed to be catching onto the concept, but wondered if dealing with all those feelings would distract him from football. If his performance went down, the coach wouldn't care that he was attending every practice. Drew validated those concerns, drawing parallels between the complexities of managing all kinds of relationships.

As the session wound down, Lo appeared to shift back closer to his usual self. "Thanks for talking me through this Mr. G. And thanks even more for not wearing those church shoes again!" he cackled as he got up to dap up Drew.

"I take your fashion critiques seriously, okay?" Drew laughed along as they briefly embraced.

"Hey, what's that?" Lo pointed down at the magazine sticking out of Drew's bag. "Is that a *Gamez Unlimited?*" He bent over to pick it up, disregarding any need for permission. "I didn't know you were a gamer Mr. G. I mean, a pretty old one though. You know *GU* has a website, social media, and a YouTube page. Nobody buys the magazine anymore."

"I'm not much of a gamer anymore, given how much time I spend changing the world one young mind at a time now," Drew teased. "But this is a special issue for me. There's an article in there I think might be helpful for a friend of mine. Actually, if you don't mind," he said, looking down at his watch, "I need to run to make sure I don't miss him." Drew took the magazine back from Lo and playfully used it to shoo him out of his office.

"Okay, I'll catch you later, Mr. G!" Lo's voice echoed as he angled toward the basketball court. Every now and then, Drew would see him in there either putting up shots or acting as a blocking machine against the younger kids.

Taking a moment to gather himself, Drew flipped through the magazine one more time. Doubts were starting to creep from the back of his mind, but he didn't have time to give them any attention. It was minutes after five-thirty, and he was worried he might have missed Amir already. He walked briskly to the RCC's front entrance hoping he'd planned correctly. After recovering from his hangover that weekend, he'd remembered Amir's initial email, stating that he worked near the community center. Since it was clear he wasn't going to answer any of Drew's messages, trying to intercept him on his way back from work was the best option available.

Outside, Drew looked back and forth, hoping against his better judgment that Amir might pop up out of nowhere just at the time most convenient to him. Maybe he should have been waiting outside a little earlier. He cursed at himself, dreading that if he had to wait to catch Amir next week, too much time may have passed for him to be able to make any difference. It had to happen today. He leaned against the wall, trying to be aware of each passerby without appearing creepy. Just then, a commotion down the street broke his focus.

"Watch out, ma'am!" someone shouted before the blare of a horn and screech of tires brought a car to an abrupt halt, sparing a busy-looking woman attempting to cross the street against traffic. The woman aimed a middle finger at the driver and continued on her way, stopping and starting between passing cars, clearly not deterred from reaching her destination.

The man who had tried to stop her gave a shrug to the driver. Once the car moved on, the light changed, giving the man the right of way to cross. He looked both ways, turning his body more than necessary, using the extra caution the busy woman had no use for. The man was a couple blocks down, but Drew recognized his movements having seen him walk or run away from him so many times last week. *Amir!* So, he had missed him, but not by much.

Drew broke into a jog-sprint, crossing the street at the intersection one back from where Amir was, and continued following him. Luckily, Amir was strolling slowly, so it didn't take long to catch up with him. Drew caught his breath and then called out, "Amir!"

Amir stopped and turned slightly, looking over his shoulder. As his eyes met Drew's, he huffed and started walking again.

"Amir, wait," Drew pleaded, walking up alongside him. "I'm so glad I spotted you. I was waiting outside the RCC for a while there. I thought I missed you."

"What?" Amir stopped again, his forehead tightening as he scowled at Drew. "So, first, you harassed me by email, and now you're stalking me? What did I possibly not make clear last week? Leave me alone!"

Before Amir could walk away, Drew stuck out his arm, shoving the rolled-up magazine into Amir's chest. "I just wanted to give you this." He braced himself.

Amir took the magazine, looking in puzzlement at its cover. "A *Gamez Unlimited*? What am I supposed to do with this?"

"Take a look at the bottom left corner," Drew explained.

Amir read out loud, "Interview with Manny Isaac of Mannyaac Games, by Will Peters". He stared down at his backpack strap, making the connection to the pin placed on it.

"I knew I recognized that symbol somewhere, but it didn't dawn on me until over the weekend when I stumbled upon my copy of *Finder's Keeper*." Drew had blurted this all out rather quickly, scared Amir would just tear the magazine up and walk away.

"Okay, so we're both fans of one of the most popular games from a couple years ago," Amir droned. "Like I said before, I'm not you and I don't want to be you. This proves you weren't listening."

"Just read it. Please." Drew clapped his hands together in feigned prayer. "It will make sense once you do. If not, I'll turn right back around and you'll never see or hear from me again."

Amir sighed heavily. "Alright."

Tale #7: Creative Control

By: Will Peters

Prodigy. Visionary. Innovator.

Twenty-year-old independent game developer, Manny Isaac, has had all these labels cast on him since releasing his debut action-thriller, *Finder's Keeper*, last year. Despite the fanfare, the industry hasn't heard much from the founder of Mannyaac Games himself. His ability to maintain a low profile makes his success that much more impressive. Blockbuster games with massive budgets and legions of loyal, online players have dominated sales for the better part of the last decade, so watching a solo indie developer rack up more first week sales than the latest installation of a storied first-person shooter franchise became the talk of social media and online forums. When given the chance to finally sit across from Isaac, the mystery maintains a veil that makes it difficult to get a read on his state of mind.

It's the morning after the annual Indie Game Awards, the ceremony dedicated to celebrating the year's top achievements in independent video game development. I'm unsure how Isaac feels about winning Developer of the Year, an unheard-of feat for a first-time solo developer and nominee. As I prep for our conversation, I see him processing a last-minute decision on which way to tie his dreads back, before ultimately letting them flow freely around his shoulders. This reflects his approach to game design, unafraid to experiment while also willing to do what makes sense in the moment. Isaac is a young man quietly confident in who he is and what he has to offer, so much so that he seems to know he doesn't have to project it.

I was expecting an interview experience full of digging and trying to get a peek behind the mask of this mysterious figure destined for a career unlike much of what we've seen before. Instead, Isaac steered us directly into a discussion of one of the most intimate parts of his life, divulging how his remarkable success was almost nothing more than a dream.

This interview has been edited for clarity.

Will Peters: I appreciate you taking the time to sit down with me. I know exposure isn't your thing. What does it feel like being the talk of the town in the gaming industry? Although it's mostly praise, is it hard to sit back and not offer your own input?

Manny Isaac: I see my work as my input. I may not put myself out there a lot or have a heavy online presence, but I'm definitely not passive about the whole thing. Between navigating the behind-the-scenes aspects of the industry and trying to maintain somewhat of a normal life, I haven't taken much time to process everything that's happened.

WP: Well, the most recent thing that's happened is winning the Developer of the Year award last night. It's historic, and there's no doubt you deserve it. Explain the work ethic needed to achieve such a great honor right at the start of your career.

MI: Honestly, I owe a lot of it to just my perspective on gaming. You see a lot of these trends where studios are basically just copying the previous year's most popular game. Or they're creating a game with no substance, only designed to make them money off in-game transactions.

I just stay true to me. It's hard to stay indie now, because these bigger companies will try to scoop up original talent in order to avoid competition. That was never a goal for me. I've always been a little different, so I can't let anyone try to mold or stifle my creativity.

WP: So, then there may be some truth to the rumor you turned down an opportunity to work for the studio you ended up outselling your first week?

MI: Sounds like a question for them (*shrugs*).

WP: Understood. On the topic of creative freedom, in your acceptance speech last night, you mentioned "barriers to [your] creativity" you had to overcome. You burst onto the scene so quickly, you seem to have leaped right over anything in your way. Tell me what you meant.

MI: I guess that's an easy assumption to make. When people only see the end result and are so impressed by it, they tend to overlook where creators start from.

WP: You're right. What you've created is unlike anything the industry has seen in a long time. But since we don't know your story, there's a lot of blanks to fill in. So, what was it that held back your creative process at first?

MI: It actually goes back to I guess my sophomore year in high school. This was around the time when my interest in games had changed from just playing them to wanting to make them. [*Pauses*] It's hard to figure out where to start with this story. Basically, when I was about sixteen years old, a situation almost put my life on an entirely different path. At the time, my mom and I were constantly fighting and I wasn't really big on school; I would skip class with friends and sometimes come home real late at night. One night I…

Here, Isaac stares blankly, seemingly unaware he has trailed off.

WP: If we need to take a break, we can. No pressure to continue with the story either.

MI: No, it's fine. One night, I snuck out of the house to go hang with some friends. As I was sneaking back through my bedroom window, my mom was there waiting for me. My brother had snitched. I got into a big fight with him and ended up throwing a vase at the wall. My mom thought that was reason enough to call the cops and tell them I was experiencing a "crisis." Long story short, they showed up along with an ambulance and I got taken to the psych ward. They ended up diagnosing me with bipolar disorder.

WP: Wow. That's a big disclosure to make publicly. I appreciate you being open enough to do so. I'm sensing there's a lot more to this story, but are you feeling okay to talk about it?

MI: It's better if people know. Like you said, the industry hasn't had much to go on to tell my story. Now that I'm able to tell it, I want to tell it all.

WP: This all didn't happen too long ago. How did you react to your diagnosis, and how has your understanding of it changed over the last few years?

MI: I didn't really get what the doctors were telling me, at first. All I knew was, I didn't want to stay in the hospital. Once my mom agreed to let them give me meds, the stay didn't really last that long, but neither of us realized our real issues were just beginning.

WP: I'm no expert, but I know some have had the experience of medications hindering their creativity. Did that happen to you? Was that the barrier you had to overcome?

MI: They did slow me down a bit, but I didn't stay on them long. Actually, I never should have been prescribed them since my mom and I later found out I was misdiagnosed. That mistake was the real barrier to everything. Because of how I was labeled, my future was called into question. During the short time I was hospitalized, I talked to lots of hospital staff, including the psychiatrist who ran the ward. She spoke to my mom and I maybe twice, but not for more than fifteen minutes each time. Based off only those few conversations, I received my diagnosis.

WP: That easily? Did it seem like other patients in the hospital received more attention?

MI: I don't think so. It was pretty packed in there, so the doctor's schedule was legitimately tight. Not to excuse the decisions she made, of course. The assumptions she made about me were terrible. See, like I mentioned, my interest in making games was just beginning to blossom. I had only told my mom about it recently, and she thought it was part of the reason I was skipping school at the time.

Now, the psychiatrist was saying bipolar disorder would make it impossible for me to even get into college, much less to work in the video game industry. It was "beyond my capacity." She even said that my desire to create a video game was an example of grandiose thinking, a bipolar symptom.

WP: Wait, wait. So, a sixteen-year-old aspiring to make video games was a sign of grandiosity? I mean, had this psychiatrist met a teenager before?

MI: Exactly. It's not like I said I wanted to become a billionaire game developer overnight or anything like that. I just had the dream to create. And not to mention, my mom had to hear someone tell her that her son wouldn't amount to anything and should only be seen as a problem to control.

WP: How long were things like this? What eventually changed?

MI: It was a few months until we found a therapist. My mom strongly preferred I work with a Black male therapist, so we waited until we found one. And he turned out to be our saving grace. Shout out to Mr. Cal!

WP: There still aren't too many Black male therapists out there, trust me, I've tried to find one myself. You were pretty lucky.

MI: Yeah. First, I want people to know that my experience in the hospital was just one example of what many of us go through. In certain ways, there's validity to concerns in Black communities about going to see a mental health professional. What my mom did by having me hospitalized was intended to help me but ended up being harmful, though it could have been much worse. We *were* lucky. Starting therapy with Cal was amazing, not just because he looked like me. It was the shared experience and understanding of where Black people exist in American society that was so important. In my first session with him, he requested to see the full written assessment detailing my bipolar diagnosis. I don't think my mom and I even thought to ask for this from the hospital, and it was never offered, which just goes to show how interested they were in my care. So, we gave him the assessment and after reviewing it, he showed us in the next session some parts that stood out to him. In addition to the part about my "grandiose thinking," the assessment was littered with interpretations he explained as being influenced by racial bias. He said my experience fell in line with a long history of misdiagnosing Black people based on racist perceptions of us being violent, threatening, unintelligent, and a host of other negative traits. He added that the mental health care system is so heavily informed by Eurocentric theories and practices, that people from different cultures have their behaviors taken out of context or crammed into boxes to fit diagnostic labels.

WP: The diagnosis, then, was a sort of misunderstanding. A cultural one. Do you feel lucky to have run into a therapist so knowledgeable?

MI: In a way, yes. The reason I remember what he said so well is because he didn't treat my mom and I like we were ignorant. He wasn't full of himself and his "expertise." He built a relationship with us based on respect and ensured we understood how we had been misguided by the system. From there, he also reframed the conflict between my mom and I as a struggle over independence, common to adolescence, and helped us work through that. He also recommended a local program for teens interested in video games that taught some of the basics of game design and branding. He leaned into my dream instead of snatching it away from me.

WP: Interesting. So, you stayed in therapy?

MI: Yup. Diagnosis or not, I was a teenager coming into my own. I know I grew a lot from being in therapy. It helped solidify a lot of the self-confidence I have today.

WP: This was a life changing experience for you in so many ways. You made it over the hurdle and you're here now. Do you see yourself becoming more of a mental health advocate as you continue your gaming career?

MI: I'm glad to be able to help, even in my own small way. With my story out there now, maybe people can relate it to their own experiences. I feel like it's a big responsibility to be an advocate, but mental health is extremely important and our conversations tend to tiptoe around the intersections with race and negative experiences people may have when seeking help. I'm all for bringing a perspective that challenges the status quo. It's kinda my thing.

WP: What do you want people to take away from your story?

MI: What I hope people can take from my story is the willingness to trust their instincts. I mean that in different ways. When it comes to seeking help, stay informed and ask questions. I've learned that that's okay. My experience taught me it's in my best interest to know how someone, no matter how many degrees they have, is viewing me and if they understand the impact they can have on my life. Also, you have to trust yourself when pursuing your dreams. For all the kids out there, keep going. For the adults around them, provide support. My experience may have been extreme in some ways, but it's really important not to knock a kid's dream or place doubt on them because you think it's unrealistic. Everybody deserves the chance to offer their gifts to the world.

CHAPTER
NINE

Drew watched Amir's eyes go wide at a certain point while reading the interview. Hopefully, he'd noticed what Drew intended him to.

Amir looked up from the magazine when he was done reading. "Wait a minute, was the therapist named Cal that Manny mentioned your friend?"

Drew smiled, thankful Amir was able to remember his friend's name out of all the stories he'd told him last week. "Yes! I'm glad I kept a copy of the magazine. They had taken his name out of the article when the digital issue was published, so I knew you would need a little more proof than just me telling you he was Manny's therapist."

"I mean, it could still be a different Cal, but I believe you," Amir responded dryly. "Either way, what is this supposed to prove to me? I don't keep up with the behind-the-scenes of the game industry, so it was cool getting to know more of Manny's story, I guess, but I don't get why you chased me down for this." He handed the magazine back to Drew.

"Right. I didn't have much time to explain once I caught up to you. The article's supposed to show you that there are successful outcomes in the mental health field. Not success like, 'Hey, my friend provided therapy to a well-known game designer'." A passerby on the sidewalk glanced over at Drew as he said this. "Do you mind if we head back to the RCC while we talk, Amir? There are too many people around to speak freely."

Amir sucked his teeth, rolling his head back in frustration.

"I promise I won't keep you as long as last time," Drew offered.

"Let's make it quick. I got lots of homework to catch up on," Amir said as he started to walk ahead of Drew.

Drew thanked the heavens he'd managed to avoid resistance. He kept his voice low as he continued explaining while matching Amir's stride. "What I mean is, Cal was able to help a family see how they had been wronged by the mental health system and successfully redirected the course they were on so that they had a positive outcome in the end." He didn't see anything change in Amir's presence to suggest his words were making an impact. The pair crossed back over the street, silence hanging between them.

"Look, I know I was wrong last week," Drew admitted. "All I did was focus on negative experiences I've had and made it sound like that's all there is to look forward to in this field. I'm sorry for doing that, and I'm ashamed I pushed you away from your dream. There's nothing wrong with continuing your family's legacy. How's your mom doing by the way?"

Finally, something shifted in Amir's demeanor. "Well, that was a little better than your rambling email apologies."

Drew stared down at the sidewalk, still embarrassed by his actions over the weekend. "Sorry about that, too."

"And my mom's condition is becoming stable," Amir noted. "Not better, but not worse. I'll take that for now." He nodded his head downward with a finality suggesting he didn't want to share anymore.

Drew could only imagine how much was on Amir's mind. He was glad now they'd had the week apart. With time to reconsider his outlook, Drew knew he could be mindful of the weight Amir was carrying.

"When I think about what happened last week, it's kind of sad," Drew began. "I told myself I was going to be this great resource to young Black men wanting to become therapists, but I was stuck just in the recruitment process. It wasn't until I met you that I realized my own underlying motive for starting the group. My true aim wasn't just to help others get into this field; it was to make myself feel like everything I'd been through was worth it. Your own story reminded me how strongly I was affected in those early years, and I just couldn't let you go through the same thing."

They came to a stop at the doors to the RCC. Amir still appeared unimpressed. "Yeah, I remember. I was there."

"I got so caught up in those stories, trying to prove my point, I overlooked the most obvious fact," Drew said. "I'm still a counselor! Clearly, despite all the bad that happened I decided to stick with it. Which is why I wanted to bring you back here." Amir gave an exasperated expression, impatiently waiting for Drew to go on.

"This place," Drew started as he swung open the doors, "was pivotal in me finding a way to make this career sustainable for me." They walked through the lobby as Drew continued. "Following all the challenges I faced in the first five years of being a counselor, I thought it was already time for me to quit. I was overwhelmed, burned out, and confused about how I had so quickly fallen out of love with the thing I had planned to dedicate my life to. It took some time, but I eventually found a way to keep going."

Rounding the corner, Lo and another boy who looked a couple years younger than him were locked in a discussion about the basketball game that just finished.

"Nah, you saw how I hit that fadeaway on you," Lo bragged. "You know I don't even play basketball too much; just admit it, I'm nice!"

The other boy rejected Lo's self-assessment, explaining how he had slipped when trying to block Lo's shot.

Lo spotted Drew as they passed each other. "Hey, Mr. G, since these little boys can't handle me, you and me gotta play one-on-one next week, okay? Give me a bit of a challenge at least."

"I'll think about it," Drew responded with a laugh.

Turning back to Amir, he continued as they walked toward his office. "I was ready to call it quits until I happened to stumble upon a new program the city government had launched. They were starting a violence interruption program, targeted at youth who were at risk of becoming involved in neighborhood violence. To ensure positive outcomes for the program, the city was offering grants to pay therapists to provide free mental health services to the teens involved. The RCC is where I started to come once a week to work with them."

"How did that keep you interested in counseling?" Amir asked. "Seems like you're still working with a lot of trauma and stuff."

"That's true, but by taking the initiative to craft my work in a way that was meaningful for me, I took back control. A lot of my friends got put in juvie when I was young. This felt like a way for me to break the cycle in the next generation. The sense of purpose I experienced in this role inspired me to leave the community-based agency job I was in at the time and open a private practice of my own. I found that my biggest problem was feeling bogged down by structures I was trying to squeeze myself into. Of course, there's still rules and regulations to follow, but I don't have to compromise my values now."

"Sounds pretty lucky," Amir started as they approached Drew's office. Drew jiggled his keys in the doorknob a few times before it cranked open. "What if you hadn't found this opportunity?"

"I think another would have come along," Drew answered. "What's most important was the shift in mindset I experienced. It wasn't just the result of my individual will-power. I can explain more, but it will take another story."

Amir rolled his eyes. "I can't do this again. I gotta go."

"I promise this is the last one," Drew said, motioning for Amir to sit. "No doom and gloom, I swear."

Amir sat on the arm of the chair in the corner, perched and ready to bounce out of the room at a moment's notice. "Go ahead, man."

TALE #8: MEN OF RESPONSIBILITY

The smell of meat and melted cheese met me as I rounded the booth to the area of tables arranged in the middle of the restaurant. Not patient enough to wait, Cal and Brandon were already digging into the pile of chili cheese fries, only looking up when I dragged a chair back from the table. They both mumbled what I assumed were apologies through stuffed mouths before wiping their hands off and standing up to greet me.

I embraced them each with a hug, then sat down to enjoy what was left of the appetizer. It was good to see the guys again. Both of them moved out of the city after graduation, coming back to visit individually as they could, but the three of us hadn't been together in the five years following school. The restaurant was one we frequented during our Master's program; it was close to campus and had quality food along with inexpensive drinks.

Cal was the one who suggested we meet there for dinner. Even after graduation, he'd maintained that aura of someone I looked up to, so I didn't mind that he often felt like the unnamed "leader" of our trio. "Glad you could make it, man," he said with a smile. "I thought meeting in your city at a familiar spot would make it easy for you to get here, but we couldn't wait any longer to get our usual appetizer."

"Sorry about that," I said, heaping a load of fries onto my plate. "Work's been a lot lately. And you know it's not really a nine to five, so I couldn't just cut my last session short."

"You get paid overtime?" Brandon asked with a raised eyebrow.

"Tuh," I scoffed. "You know it's not like that at these agencies. I gotta get those billable hours however I can, if I want to keep my job that is."

"Man, that's trash," Brandon responded.

I turned my hand up in a half shrug. "No argument over here." The waiter stopped by to get our drink orders and to tell me about the specials on the menu he'd already explained to the other two. "Enough about work though, what's been going on with you guys?"

They both gave some updates about how life was treating them, but it seemed halfhearted. Even Brandon's mention of meeting a woman he saw a potential future with fell flat, as if his own excitement was forced or his mind was on other things.

"Okay, is there something I missed before I got here?" I asked. "Am I not in on the joke? You guys sound like robots. Are you reading off a teleprompter behind me or am I losing it?" I looked over my shoulders exaggeratedly, trying to break up whatever routine they were doing.

Cal looked at me with a smile; not a jovial one though, still looking like he knew something I didn't. Brandon could only look down at the empty plate in front of him. The waiter returned with our drinks and took our dinner orders.

"No, you're not losing it, bro'," Cal said.

"Or, maybe you are. That's what we're trying to figure out," Brandon added, obviously upsetting Cal given his facial expression. Brandon simply responded with a self-assured shrug.

"Yo, what are you guys talking about?" I asked, with some extra edge added to my exasperation.

Cal answered first. "Look, of course I wanted us all to get together to have a good time; catch up and what not. But, at the same time I'm worried. We both are." He looked at Brandon who nodded in agreement. "We're five years into this thing, and every time we hear from you about work, it seems like there's another issue."

I couldn't believe what I was hearing. "Wait, so you got us together to get on me for complaining about work?" I asked.

"No, no, not at all," Cal replied. "We all know that work in general can be a pain: bosses, policies, forced birthday celebrations no one asked for." He and Brandon chuckled, but not me. "Our line of work is different, though. There's so much we have to take in. Sometimes, people's lives are in our hands. Any outside distractions make all of that harder."

Brandon elaborated. "Yeah, it sounds like you just keep running into incident after incident where people either aren't understanding your position as a Black man or are just being straight up racist. Sometimes it sounds like you don't even want to do this anymore. Do you?" He asked the question as if he already knew the answer. I did too. I couldn't pretend like it was the first time I'd thought about it. I just didn't realize I'd made it so obvious to my friends in our conversations.

My defensiveness got to me first. "Don't act like you guys haven't told me about having similar experiences. I only tell you so much because I know you can relate. Hell, we all met in grad school, so I know you remember—"

"The professor mixing up our names," we all said in unison.

"Of course," Cal continued. "We're not saying we've somehow graduated from the Black experience; we just want to make sure it isn't breaking you. So, what's really going on?"

Our food arrived, but I couldn't find my appetite anymore. I felt a sinking sensation in my stomach as I recalled various events from my time as a therapist so far. Times when I felt ignored, disrespected, and unappreciated. "It's…it's been hard." I looked up at the ceiling, holding back tears. "I don't understand how I got here. Why is it that I've been so hurt by this field when all I'm trying to do is help?"

The weight of the question fell on all three of us. Cal and Brandon looked deep in thought. I felt bad for changing the mood of the table, but they were the ones who asked for me to open up.

"I'm sorry things have gone this way, man," Brandon finally broke the silence. "Even though we've talked through different problems, I had no idea the real depth of how you felt."

"I appreciate you coming clean," Cal added. "Your honesty is a gift. From the time we met, you've always wanted to tell it like it is. Now, it might not have always been at the right times," Brandon nodded along with a soft, reminiscing smile, "but it's needed. And to see you put in a position where you might give this all up hurts me too."

"Yeah, it's not right what you've had to deal with," Brandon added.

In that moment, I felt grateful to have quality friends. How many people could depend on their friends to validate and support them in a time of need? What happened as our conversation progressed showed me how much they cared, how they were able to see through the fog for me and show me a path toward what lay beyond what I could imagine for myself.

"Think about how much we're carrying," Cal said. His words made me notice my slouch. I straightened my posture almost out of respect. "Personally and professionally. As Black men in this field, it's important for us to determine what burdens we actually have the responsibility to hold and what we can let go of." He looked around with certainty that what he was saying was the undeniable truth.

"I know that's right," Brandon said. "The clinical and ethical practices are enough to keep up with. Then you realize this job everyone says is so important doesn't make you financially secure overnight. And on top of that we still gotta be Black and navigate the same mess as some of our clients? Nah."

It all rang true to me. "I guess I've been holding onto perceptions. Trying to be what this profession says I should be, and trying to do everything I can to help our people. We're needed, right?" So much of my stress came from the pressure to be what everyone wanted from me. I knew it was impossible, but it didn't stop me from trying.

"Yes, of course we are," Cal answered. "And because of that, again, we need to know who we're responsible to and what we're responsible for. You gotta sort that out before anything else."

"Well, I wish I could just do things my way, but I'd probably end up out of a job," I said.

Cal shook his head. "Not what I mean. Look at us sitting here. For starters, we're all men in a field where there's not many of us, and men don't even go to therapy that much. We're responsible for challenging that reality. Boys and men receive so many messages telling us to be strong by hiding our emotions, of course we don't want to talk about them. We're never given the space to!"

"And we know those expectations are stronger for Black men," Brandon stated. "Along with everything else we go through."

"I agree. That's one of the main reasons why I do this," I explained. "I want to provide Black boys with the space to process their experiences, from the traumatic to the joyous, so they'll be able to confront this world that's designed to break them down."

Brandon nodded. "Remember too, it's not our job to save people. Like you just said, this world is set up to be against us. Therapy by itself can't break down these systems, so we can't take on all that responsibility. There's work for everybody to do."

"It's hard not to though," I responded. "Their pain is my pain. I want to be there for them."

"You won't be if you keep submitting to others' wishes for you," Brandon said, matter-of-factly.

"That's what I'm talking about," Cal said. "We all have a purpose in this field. Once you find it, you have to stick to it. Let your values guide you, that way you don't veer off course at every obstacle. At the same time, know that your path might take shape in ways you don't expect. I just started working with a teenage client who wants to make video games. It never occurred to me until I met him how much I enjoy encouraging others' creativity. Now, I can develop that into a specialty."

I understood Cal's point, but I still felt stuck. What was I supposed to do? "So, basically, if I let my values guide me, I'll find my way out of this situation and into something better."

Brandon adjusted his glasses. "Who knows what else might happen; you can't predict everything. If you keep what's most important first though, you'll be able to tell when things aren't going the right way much sooner."

I let everything sink in as we finished our meal. While I might have preferred us having a normal dinner, I couldn't have been more grateful for how it went. Adopting a new mindset wouldn't change how I was feeling right away; I really was experiencing some harmful work environments. My hope was that I'd at least be able to redirect my focus to the future and how I could craft it to my liking, rather than being bogged down in my current surroundings. After all, I still had responsibilities to fulfill, in my own way.

CHAPTER

TEN

"YOU SHOULD HAVE STARTED WITH THAT STORY LAST WEEK. I might not have been so mean." Amir had settled onto the chair's cushion, more attentive than had seemed possible when Drew convinced him to return to the RCC.

"Well, you know, I prefer to project my work-based trauma onto people. I find that it's pretty inviting." It felt good for Drew to trade light-hearted jokes with Amir. After feeling like an opportunity had walked away from him forever, redemption felt closer.

"I'm still a little lost, though," Amir said. "I get that your friends helped you pivot in your career, but I'm still a college student. How does the lesson apply to my life?"

"Sounds like a question for a mentor," Drew replied. "Does this mean you're interested in the group again?" He cringed as soon as he said it; he was being too eager.

"We don't have to go over this again," Amir said. "You know what my motivation is, so if you can make this group worth my while and not shame me away from my goals, I'm down." He looked sincere. Both about how much Drew had hurt him and his willingness to give him another chance.

Drew took the words as seriously as they were said. There was no guarantee he wouldn't make another mistake, of course, but he knew what direction he was going in now.

"Thanks, Amir. That means a lot to me. Really. I'm aware now that I can't push you or any other mentees in the direction I want you to go. All I can do is provide information, good or bad. Think of it like this: when someone's selling a used car, it's wrong for them not to tell potential buyers about the car's history, like accidents or needed maintenance. With the right information though, the buyer can make a careful decision and decide if they're up to putting in the work to make the car function how they need it to. Basically, it's still my responsibility to warn you about the difficulties inherent to the mental health field, but there are ways to navigate it in a way that's sustainable and fits your personal goals." It was a messy metaphor, but he figured another story might reverse all the progress he'd made with Amir.

Amir tilted his head. "I think I follow you. I mean, to be honest, it's not like I just forgot all the bad stories you told me last week. When I got back to my dorm I was still pissed, but they stuck with me. The vicarious trauma, how people talk about clients behind their backs, even that little Harold and Gerald parable you made up. They all gave me something to think about."

Drew was somewhat surprised to hear him admit this. "Guess I can keep some of those in the group curriculum then. As far as a start date, I think I'll still be able to do it at the top of next semester. I'll plan to rework my pitch and reach back out to the students I spoke to already to see if they're still willing to join."

"Sounds good, Mr. G." Amir hopped up, excitedly moving to exit Drew's office. "I'll be on the lookout for more details once you get everything ready. Just no emails after midnight, okay?"

Drew shook Amir's hand out in the hallway. "Thanks, Amir. I know I'm supposed to be the mentor, but I've learned a lot from you already. I hope to be able to provide what you need to grow into the best representation of your dreams."

"I look forward to learning what it takes to be a counselor like you. Flaws and all." Amir left the RCC, this time leaving Drew reassured about the mentoring group.

A deep exhale soothed the tension Drew had been holding onto for a week. "I saw all that." Tina was leaning on the wall outside her office, looking at Drew with an expression that said she was reluctantly impressed. "So whatever trick you had in your bag worked, huh?"

"Turned out it wasn't so much the trick as just me being honest," Drew explained. "Amir's going to join the mentoring group, and I'm planning on re-contacting the guys I spoke to previously to see if they're still interested."

"I'm glad it all worked out," Tina said. "Even though I'm not in your sessions, I can tell how much of an impact you've had on the kids you work with here. I can only assume you'll do the same for these college students."

Drew was grateful that he and the youth at the RCC had someone like Tina supporting them. "Thanks, Tina. You've always had my back. You know, once this group starts, I might be too busy to reply to all your texts—"

"Don't even start, Drew." Tina drifted back toward her office, commending him again.

OVER THE NEXT COUPLE OF DAYS, DREW GOT BACK IN TOUCH with the two students he'd met before Amir. Luckily, he had never officially rejected them, so they both accepted his offer to join the group without hesitation. He also reached out to the schools he was sourcing to give them an updated description of the group and new, looser parameters around the vetting process.

It felt like he'd emerged into the light at the end of the tunnel, and the possibilities he saw before him were encouraging. If not for meeting Amir, he didn't know what state the group would be in. Would he even have found enough students to get it off the ground? Even so, at some point his unrecognized desire to protect others from the experiences he had would have emerged. And who knows what consequences it would have had for other students.

In order to help students move forward in becoming the next generation of therapists, he now understood he'd have to look back on his career from a different angle. No one has to endure trauma and racism for the sake of a career. Still, the value of his tough lessons could only take root in others with the knowledge that there were many ways to develop a fulfilling career, as long as they used their creativity and trusted in their values.

All of this ran through Drew's mind as he planned out the group's process in detail. Just as he knew he had more tales to tell, he was ready to start others on the paths of their own stories that were yet to be written.

ABOUT THE AUTHOR

CHRIS GAMBLE IS A LICENSED PROFESSIONAL COUNSELOR IN Washington, D.C. His experiences working in the mental health field inspired him to write *Tales of a Black Therapist*, his debut novel. He strives to tell better mental health stories in order to shift the narratives shaping our systems of care. His other writing can be found in Counseling Today magazine. Follow him on Instagram @chris_thecounselor.

DISCUSSION QUESTIONS

THANK YOU FOR READING *TALES OF A BLACK THERAPIST*. THE following questions are mainly geared toward mental health professionals, but all readers are welcome to answer them as best they can. If possible, readers are encouraged to go over these questions with a group in order to deepen their exploration of the themes discussed.

1. "Mistaken Identity" and "Lucky Guess" explore experiences of racism in higher education settings. Would Drew's experiences have differed at an HBCU versus a PWI? Why or why not?

2. The limitations of the school system loom large in "A for Effort". What comes to mind when you think about the fact that some Black chil-

dren will graduate from the school system without "catching up" academically?

3. In "Shook," Drew talks about the privilege he has in not having to live in the same environment as Vince. How do issues of class complicate assumptions about shared racial experiences?

4. "Deep Roots" highlights a recurring theme of the book: how Black people are talked about and perceived, particularly in health care contexts. What strategies would you have recommended to Drew given the work situation discussed in this tale?

5. In "Two Sides of a Worthless Coin," readers are shown two different experiences of the expectations placed on Black therapists. As a Black therapist or other professional, what has been asked of you that made you feel exploited?

6. "Creative Control" spotlights the misdiagnosis of Black people in the mental health care system. What are some solutions to this problem?

7. "Men of Responsibility" discusses the burden placed on Black therapists to heal their communities. In addition to therapy, what other approaches can contribute to improving the state of Black mental health?

8. *Tales of a Black Therapist* examines the process of what it takes to exist as Black people in a profession not designed with us in mind. What is needed to make a career in mental health attractive and sustainable for Black people?